D1443465

No Ordinary Noel

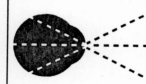

This Large Print Book carries the
Seal of Approval of N.A.V.H.

No Ordinary Noel

Pat G'Orge-Walker

THORNDIKE PRESS

A part of Gale, Cengage Learning

GALE
CENGAGE Learning·

Detroit • New York • San Francisco • New Haven, Conn • Waterville, Maine • London

LIBRARY OF CONGRESS CATALOGING-IN-PUBLICATION DATA

G'Orge-Walker, Pat.
    No ordinary noel / by Pat G'Orge-Walker. — Large print ed.
      p. cm. — (Thorndike Press large print African-American)
    "A Sister Betty Novel."
    ISBN-13: 978-1-4104-5301-3 (hardcover)
    ISBN-10: 1-4104-5301-4 (hardcover)
    1. African Americans—Fiction. 2. African American churches—Fiction. 3.
Church membership—Fiction. 4. Christian fiction, American. 5. Pelzer
(S.C.)—Fiction. 6. Large type books. I. Title.
    PS3607.O597N6 2012
    813'.6—dc23   2012030647

Published in 2012 by arrangement with Dafina Books, an imprint of
Kensington Publishing Corp.

Printed in Mexico
1 2 3 4 5 6 7 16 15 14 13 12

More than two thousand years ago, three Wise Men came from the Far East. They traveled to Bethlehem bearing gifts for the baby Jesus who lay in a manger.

Man and beast, far and wide, celebrated.

Trustee Freddie Noel also came from the East: New York City's Harlem bearing a "tainted" gift for his beloved church.

His pastor tried to beat him like a Mexican piñata.

Enjoy and Happy Holidays!

ACKNOWLEDGMENTS

For God so loved the world, that He gave
His only begotten son, that whosoever
believeth in him should not perish, but
have everlasting life

John 3:16

*On Christ the solid rock I stand, all other
ground is sinking sand.*

I remain sustained by prayers and support
from those who've become too numerous
to name. I thank them all.

I also thank with all my heart and my love,
Robert — my best friend and husband. Also
my beautiful children: Gizel Dan-Yette,
Ingrid, and Marisa along with my grand-
children, and great-grandchildren. A special
mention for the birth of my latest great-
granddaughter, Honestee Navaeh.

I am eternally grateful to my bishop
John L. Smith and Lady Laura L. Smith of
the St. Paul Baptist Tabernacle of Lights

7

Ministry, and to that congregation, Reverend Stella Mercado and the Blanche Memorial Church family, and other numerous, supportive churches and organizations.

Deep gratitude and appreciation to my editor Selena James and the Dafina/Kensington Books family; long-time friend and attorney, Christopher R. Whent, Esq.; publicist Ella Curry (EDC Creations); and Yolanda LaToya Gore — a lovely woman who formed the Sister Betty Fan Club on Facebook.

Without a doubt, thanks to my offline readers and supporters, as well as my Facebook family of readers, friends, numerous book clubs, and so many fellow authors who share prayers, encouragement, and wonderful virtual hugs. Of course, I must thank the woman who makes my phenomenal promotional items, Debra "Simply Said" Owsley.

A special thank you to Doctors Colin Powers and Sandford Dubner.

A SPECIAL MESSAGE FROM THE AUTHOR

Finally, it's been more than thirty-five years since I created Sister Betty. I've grown with this phenomenal imaginary Super Saint; laughed and cried and gotten paid. This old imaginary Super Saint has taken me places and heights I never imagined. I thank God for His trust when he placed her in my hands — I pray I never let Him down.

CHAPTER 1

For the past eight years, Reverend Leotis Tom pastored full time at Pelzer, South Carolina's Crossing Over Sanctuary church. From the moment he laid his right hand upon the Bible and promised to lead the church to holiness, he'd battled one church mess after another against the Devil and, quite often, against his congregation. The besieged reverend fasted so much for peace he hadn't gained an ounce since he accepted his position.

He'd been only thirty-three years old when installed, and so fresh out of divinity college that he'd actually believed all he needed was a few words of "thus saith the Lord" scriptures and folks would fall in line; and with a touch of his anointed hands, he expected them to fall out, too. With his youthful ignorance he'd taken the helm, but not without controversy.

When the reverend's name first came up

there was concern from one of the few remaining founding members of the church. Mother Sasha Pray Onn was in her late sixties and a tad bit neurotic. Widowed by choice was the rumor, although never proven. She'd always been the go-to church mother, the keeper of the church gossip-laced politics and all things that made the church's sanctified bus ride hazardous.

On the day when the reverend's name was laid on the sacrificial altar for pastorate, Mother Pray Onn had issues. Fired up, she had left subtlety behind and was chained to her seat in the first pew.

"He ain't been seasoned enough with trials and tribulations and some hawt church mess!" she warned. "We need a Man of God who can take a punch from ole Satan and then knows how to pray that demon back to hell without getting the church scorched! I'm telling ya, that baby preacher y'all are considering, well he ain't that man!"

The Church Board never took into consideration the old church mother might've known of which she spoke. After all, Sasha Pray Onn and her entire Hellraiser clan were Satan's first cousins, although they didn't brag about it a lot. Nevertheless, the Church Board took a risk and for the first time ignored Mother Sasha Pray Onn. It wasn't much of a risk. The old woman, by that time, had gone on a cruise.

Without the sanction of the other twenty-eleven boards, the Church Board invited the very handsome, six-foot-five Reverend Leotis Tom from nearby Anderson, South Carolina, with the ink still wet on his graduation parchment, to "bring the word." They'd also made sure it was for the fifth Sunday service. Back then and even now, folks set a limit on attending church more than four Sundays a month. Fifth Sunday remains the safest for church politics.

Even as naïve as Leotis Tom was then, he still knew that an invitation was really an audition.

When the day came, he'd arrived without a visiting preacher's usual church posse. There was no armor bearer to walk him up the three steps into the pulpit. He looked almost church-naked without some middle-aged nurse to wipe his brow or two or three Mothers to sit in the first pew and hype him and the congregation into a frenzy. Reverend Tom didn't even have a young minister-in-training to carry his Bible and his robe. Instead, he came prepared with faith and a vision from the Lord.

That Sunday morning, he'd stood at the pulpit, dressed in a black and purple, short-sleeved robe, with a modest gold cross stitched across the breastbone. His dark unruly hair was cut short. Whether on purpose or not his pecan brown muscles rippled, making his arms resemble the back of an alligator's tail splashing about.

Most folks probably couldn't remember what Reverend Tom preached that morning but the consensus was unanimous. The reverend was what the women folks and even some of the shameless men called, "hawt spiritual eye-candy who knew a little sumpthin' about the Word." The fact that the young man was single suddenly was in his favor, and most hoped that he'd never marry — unless it was to one of them.

That morning, the church's outgoing pastor, the Jheri curled and overweight Reverend Knott Enuff Money could only marinate in envy. All the time he'd been single and pastoring, he'd had to fight off the gay and the bi rumors. Reverend Tom came to church with muscular arms and no mention of a wife or a girlfriend and the congregation appeared to lose its mind.

Soon after, the conversation got around again to the urgency of selecting a pastor to take the place of Reverend Knott Enuff Money.

"We can't keep putting off getting a new

pastor," one board member pointed out after learning Reverend Tom had an open invitation to preach at another local church. "I suggest we hire him immediately."

The naysayers who attended only a few services and even less board meetings usually did what they were supposed to do when it came time to confirm anything, by saying, "No," and "Hell No!" But that time, even they went with the program, and voted on a few limitations to put into his contract should he accept their offer. They kept it simple. They'd wanted shorter sermons during football and baseball seasons, and no evening service on the night of the Stella Awards.

With agreement in place on how to regulate the pastor's preaching schedule, they hired Reverend Leotis Tom and hoped for the best. They also hoped Mother Pray Onn had a good time on her cruise because she would raise hell upon her return.

The installation service was a grand affair. Churches, big and small, bishops and pastors, the saved and the unsavory were all invited. The Reverend Leotis Tom received many accolades, and large sums of cash; someone had warned him not to accept checks unless he was prepared to pay return check fees.

The food was first rate. Several overweight sisters hit that kitchen and anointed the oven. They cooked a feast big enough to feed a third world country. Of course, the auspicious event had local newspaper and television coverage. The video would be sold during a few upcoming conferences.

There was no doubt that Crossing Over Sanctuary had a new star. Everything was wonderful until later on that evening when the young preacher rose to say a few words.

The Reverend Leotis Tom gave the customary thank you and his vision for the church and community. Then he made a promise that set everyone on notice.

"There will be no politics inside the church or outside the church. Politicians are welcome to worship, but they will not receive special favors. We will not gamble on our salvation with unholy alliances and that includes gambling of any kind. God doesn't want nor will He accept tainted money or favors!"

But that was then.

CHAPTER 2

Fall 2010

A few days after the Halloween madness crept off the radar, there was a new holiday buzz all over Pelzer. Like most of the country, Pelzer townsfolk were broke. They faced turkey-free dinners and severe Christmas giving challenges.

However, from the schoolyard to the junkyard, with the jailhouse and churches in between, they still held hope for the upcoming holiday.

They snatched down their pumpkin front door decorations and got ready for the Thanksgiving and Christmas madness. Some folk were brazen and heathen enough to have a Tom Turkey figure in a manger with a huge Santa on the front porch. The Santa even had a sack of toys thrown over his back, and a Bible in his hand.

Pelzer folk never allowed reality to derail their delusions, and the Mothers Board determined the tradition should continue. When it came time for the quarterly meeting, the first Saturday in November, craziness and chaos tore down the WELCOME sign and moved in.

Extraordinary times called for extreme measures, and no one more extreme than the Mothers Board fit the bill. It was time for the bickering fundraising heads of the board to rumble. They shared the war-mongering crown: cantankerous Mother Sasha Pray Onn and incontinence-plagued Mother Bea Blister. With Thanksgiving and Christmas coming soon, it was time to put into play one of the fundraising schemes they'd hatched.

Their plots seldom worked, but like most old hens, they just kept on hatching them.

Early on, Bea and Sasha had asked for volunteers to aid in their latest sure-to-be fiasco, but only three members signed up. Those three forced labor workers, all either over or in their sixties, were Elder Bartholomew "Batty" Brick, Brother Leon Casanova, and Trustee Freddie Noel. They came aboard because Sasha and Bea had threatened to spread untruths, beat the crap out of them, or stuff laxative-laced meals down their throats.

Elder Brick had already served time and

didn't need the rumors. Brother Casanova was scared of Bea's violent nature and Sasha's entire Hellraiser family. And malnourished-looking Trustee Noel just needed a hot home-cooked meal from anywhere with or without a laxative.

The weather held out the Saturday morning of the meeting. There was just enough of a chill in the air to chill out the old folk. The five seniors arrived at Crossing Over Sanctuary church with a combined five hundred years of senility, irregularity, and illusions of holiness.

The head of the Finance Committee, Elder Bartholomew "Batty" Brick entered first. Fellow committee members Brother Leon Casanova and Trustee Freddie Noel entered next. The men then escorted Mothers Sasha and Bea into the fellowship hall. They went to the rear of the hall and sat at one of the large tables.

The five already knew why they were there. Months ago, Bea and Sasha, referred to as BS, had suggested to Reverend Tom holding a Seniors Prom as a fundraiser. More recently, when Elder Brick slipped up and told Sasha that the church's intake had slipped dramatically, she'd suggested they come up with more ideas beyond just selling tickets to the prom.

"Okay," Sasha announced. "Batty, you lead us in a word or two of prayer so we can get started."

Elder Batty Brick jumped up quicker than his arthritis normally allowed. The over-weight, tall, olive-complexioned man with snow-white hair winced. He dropped his head, clasped his hands, and blurted as if he were preaching, "You know our hearts, Lord." He let one hand sweep over their heads. "We come asking that You take our few fishes and stale crusty bread ideas and help us make some money with them."

All raised their eyes and palms toward the ceiling, and added, "Amen."

"We don't hafta read the minutes. We can just move on." The suggestion came from Mother Bea Blister.

Bea had been the Vice President of the Mothers Board for more years than she could remember. She'd also been Sasha's rival for anything she figured Sasha wanted. In her late sixties, so she said, Bea was a statuesque woman. She had a severely arched back, an extra hundred pounds, was dark as a sun-ripened raisin, and just as wrinkled.

She made her wishes known on her way out the hall to the bathroom. She'd felt an urge to go since she'd left home. Since there were men at the meeting, and she wasn't too sure if she could depend on the Depend she'd worn, it was as good a time as any to take care of business. The last thing she wanted was to be embarrassed, and definitely not with blabber-mouth Sasha present.

By the time Bea returned, she found the other four seated just as she'd left them. "What did I miss?"

"When did you leave?" Sasha asked. She'd never tell Bea that she'd held up the meeting until she returned. There was no fun in that.

That set the tone for the rest of the meeting.

"I think we should sell T-shirts," Sasha suggested, "We'll have ones printed for the men, GOT AN XTRA BLUE PILL? For the women, ME & MY BREASTS R SOUTHERN GALS."

Sasha's suggestion caught Brother Leon's attention. Up till then, he'd been dozing. He leaned forward, his brow furrowed. His seventy-year-old cinnamon-colored cheeks appeared full as if he'd stowed away a few nuts instead of sitting among them. "Ahem," he said as he pulled on his gray handlebar moustache to give his coming words more weight.

"As I see it" — he looked around to make sure all eyes were upon him — "this hall holds about five hundred people comfortably. Since we're having a throwback to the fifties, sixties, and seventies dress theme for the prom, I'm sure most won't need to do anything but look in their closets and grab something to wear. Afros, conks, platform shoes, we all got some old clothes somewhere."

"Bea can wear what she wore last Sunday." Sasha chuckled. Her tiny parentheses-shaped legs spread and, of course, she'd forgotten her underwear again.

"And Sasha can just wear what she's wearing now," Bea shot back, "except she can add drawers."

One moment Sasha's knees were open and the next the springs to Sasha's knees shut hard enough to crack a bone. She grabbed her cane and was about go Darth Vader on Bea.

Brother Casanova jumped between them, "Ladies, please. Don't make me hafta use my Taser!" He'd heard that line on television and was glad it worked. He shook his head and sighed at their pettiness as they retreated. "Anyway, we're supposed to come up with ways to make money without going over the five-hundred dollar budget. Won't

22

it cost most of that to get the shirts printed?"

Sasha didn't like her idea challenged, and she could almost feel her tight gray bun tighten. It threatened to cut off the oxygen to her brain, but she remained cool. "Of course, I already thought about that," she lied. "Bea is gonna handwrite every word on every T-shirt."

"What the ham and cheese!" Bea's spine almost straightened as she shot forward, her fists balled to strike. "Oh, forget a Ta—"

Sasha quickly cut her off when she added sweetly, "Bea has such lovely penmanship. Why should we pay for something that will have less quality?"

Bea's fist stopped in mid-air. She hadn't gone to college, but when Sasha put it that way, how could she refuse? "I do have good penmanship," Bea said with as much sincerity as an old con artist could muster. "How many T-shirts would we need?"

Elder Batty started counting on his fingers and when he added both knees to the count, he said, "Bea, I think we've sold about one hundred and fifty tickets with about two hundred more promised."

From the end of the table, someone spoke up and offered a semblance of common sense. "We do remember the Seniors Prom is the Saturday after Thanksgiving, don't

23

we? That's less than a month away. It won't leave us much time."

Everyone turned to face Trustee Freddie Noel. Until that moment, they'd not heard a peep from the tall, lemon yellow, skinny man with squinty brown eyes, and a sharp nose that looked like a carrot stick. Not only was he very tall, but extremely unattractive. In his mid-sixties, he was so thin, he'd almost had to pin his pants to his skin to keep them up.

"It'll be enough time if we're not distracted," Elder Batty Brick replied. "So you can pencil that in your notes as a done deal."

The trustee shuddered a bit. He knew that Elder Batty Brick had only mentioned the word pencil because behind his back folks called him "Number two," saying he resembled a number two pencil with a chewed eraser.

"That reminds me," Brother Casanova added, as he turned to Trustee Noel, "we haven't assigned a job to you for that night."

"Let him take the coats," Bea snapped.

Bea always dismissed Trustee Noel because he didn't fit what she looked for in a man, a congregation member, or a potential helpmate. He was too thin, too poor, and she didn't think he could stand up to the job of giving her what she'd need. "Unless

24

you're bringing a date or plan on having any fun, I don't think you'd mind taking the coats, would you?"

Before the trustee could respond Sasha added fuel to the fire, "He's celibate. Everyone knows he ain't never been married. I've never seen him dance and if he could, I'm certain he would. He ain't trying to have fun."

"Well, I'm certain he'll celebrate when he's no longer a celibate." Somehow Elder Batty Brick thought he'd helped the reclusive trustee, especially when he added, "I'm sure he's just waiting on a woman who'd have him."

As usual, the trustee's manhood always fed the gossip fire and if he wasn't weird enough for their chatter, he had a bad habit. The trustee had a sprig of silver hair resembling a half moon that peeked out from the crown of his head. Whenever he was nervous, which was most of the time, he twirled that sprig. When they finished berating him, the top of his head look like silver twigs.

They decided that Elder Batty Brick would collect the monies despite having once served time for embezzlement. Brother Casanova would DJ, even though he'd warned them about his hearing loss in one ear. He'd also supervise the hall decora-

25

tions. Sasha would oversee the food and a possible senior date auction. Bea would print by hand all the T-shirts and secure the adult entertainment.

The way they figured, even though Reverend Tom authorized only five hundred dollars for the entire affair, they'd make it work and have money to spare. Still delusional, they ended in prayer.

CHAPTER 3

Sunday, the day after the Seniors Prom committee met, nothing much changed but the weather.

The howling winter winds came earlier than expected, screaming their blizzard warnings. Torrential rains pounded the ground, leaving muddy puddles in its wake. Of course, weather was always unpredictable as were life's ups and downs. That was expected. What wasn't, however, were the storms of life that could stop everything in its tracks.

That morning a tempest brewed inside the mind of Crossing Over Sanctuary's Reverend Leotis Tom and there was no shelter other than prayer. Inside his modest town house bedroom, he lay awake with sadness in his eyes. He looked toward the ceiling and prayed. "Father God, my faith looks up to Thee. I know You will not abandon Your son . . ."

It was the same prayer he'd repeated for the past few days, seemingly more to convince himself than anything else. So that Sunday morning, rather than just lay there, the reverend slid from under the heavy dark comforter wrapped about his body like a cocoon. Looking into the bedroom mirror, he faced two startling facts that had caused him to lay awake and pray throughout much of the night before. One was that a terrible thunderstorm threatened to arrive soon and drench Pelzer and its surrounding areas. The other was when later that morning he announced that the church had a severe financial crisis, the congregation just might storm him, too. With Thanksgiving and Christmas coming in a few weeks, the announcement could not come at a worse time.

Reverend Tom turned his face to a nearby wall. "Lord, did I misunderstand? If I did, then why did you send Sister Betty as a witness to the vision three years ago?"

He had many questions for God. His community development vision project was in jeopardy. And where was his spiritual prayer warrior, Sister Betty?

Those were the same questions he'd asked God ever since he received unwelcomed news from the Piece of Savings Bank a few weeks ago. The bank had called in its option to receive the balance of the monies owed for the church's Promised Land development deal for the vacant ten acres across the highway from Crossing Over Sanctuary. If the church didn't pay then it was legally liable to forfeit whatever monies had already been invested. All improvements made on the property would also be lost.

It took all the strength he had but eventually the reverend showered and dressed for that morning's service. He opted for an off-the-rack suit rather than one tailor-made. He didn't eat, not because he was fasting, but because he had no appetite for food, or for what he had to do.

In all the years he'd preached and shared God's prophetic visions, neither his faith nor his reputation had ever taken such a hit. He'd not allowed it, especially in the wake of so many huge church scandals. He could only wonder where God's favor was now that he needed it so badly.

Bad weather and howling winds matched the reverend's mood for that Sunday's morning service. The wind and violent rain pellets shook the church's stained glass panes like a baby's rattle and mocked the reverend's heartfelt attempt at worship and praise.

He preached what he hoped was a powerful sermon from his prepared text, "Be Ye Anxious for Nothing." He whipped the congregation into worship frenzy and prayed that the Holy Ghost would prepare them for the bad news. The congregation amened, praised, and shouted. Finally, when he thought the spiritual atmosphere was ready, he spread his arms wide and indicated the people should sit. He glanced over toward the Board of Trustees and the Finance Committee because several already knew what was about to happen. The men on the board nodded slightly, urging him to step into the furnace as Daniel had.

Flames of malcontent were about to singe the faith of the Reverend Leotis Tom and the church to its core.

He lifted a square collection box from among several props he'd earlier arranged on the pulpit lectern. Reverend Tom held the box in the air and asked, "Who among you still believe God cannot be confined to a small box, no matter how hard we've always tried to keep Him there?"

Like popcorn, hands shot up, the choir broke out singing, "Our God is An Awesome God," and hallelujahs rang out in response.

He'd gotten the reaction he wanted. With a big grin and a false sense of returning peace, he started to walk peacock-proud, strutting back and forth across the front of the altar. "That's what I'm talking about," he said, as he raised an arm indicating the congregation should shut off their powerful affirmations.

"Well, for those whose faith wavers I guess I'm about to say what they'd call bad news."

No sooner had he let the words *bad news* leave his mouth than it became so quiet the reverend swore he heard a fly land on a cotton ball. Heads nodded in his direction, mostly from the Board of Trustees and the Finance Committee; an indication he should hurry up and continue before he lost his edge and their waning support.

Reverend Tom's smile stayed glued to his face as he continued to speak. "You know Satan can't just get up any time he wants and mess with the people of God. . . ."

Brother Leon Casanova, who'd slept through much of the service but didn't think anyone noticed, jumped up with his fists in the air. He twirled them as though he were in a boxing ring, warming up. "That's right, Satan. Mama said, 'knock yo butt out!' "

Reverend Tom and most of the congregation broke into laughter, seeming to forget the bad news was still to come.

"Amen, Brother Casanova." Reverend Tom turned off his laughter and replaced it with his signature defiant smile that looked more like a sneer. "Now when the Devil wanted to torment Job he had to get permission from God. In fact, not only did God give the Devil permission but it was He that first made the suggestion . . ."

"Quit stalling, Reverend," a husky, angry voice broke out from the back of the sanctuary. "We already know that Job went through a whole lotta hell. So now what the heck are you trying to tell us? What's this bad news?"

Whoever asked the question had kept their seat. It didn't matter because the reverend couldn't backtrack had he wanted to. That Job scriptural fact had the ears and the attention of the entire church. Even the usual chatterboxes seated on the we-come-every-so-often back pews shut their judgmental mouths as they stuffed their offering envelopes back into their pockets.

The half smile slid from the reverend's face and his shoulders seemed to droop as he slowly began the awful truth.

"Several weeks ago, the Finance Committee, Church Board, and I received notice from the Piece of Savings Bank. The bank is calling in the loan. It appears that Crossing Over Sanctuary can't cross over onto our Promised Land development deal as agreed. We're broke."

Although it took a few minutes for the revelation to sink in, it was more than enough time for all hell to break loose. And at that very moment, Hell was making its way off the hot seat and out of the second pew. Its small yet shrill voice cracking the already confused atmosphere was determined to have its say.

Mother Sasha Pray Onn wasn't privy to the financial difficulty, yet heard the word *broke* and that got her all riled up. As small as she was, she became an unnatural force of nature all by itself, with rimless reading glasses that bounced upon her tiny button nose. With strength she didn't know she had, those parentheses-shaped legs sprang into action.

"Hallelujah and thank you Lord, you saved me when you did!" Mother Sasha Pray Onn, Satan's sometime right-hand gal and first cousin, screamed out.

She adjusted her latest set of dentures with a loud tongue click as she made her way off her seat and along the second row of red cushioned pews.

Never one to apologize or say, "Excuse me," she used her ever-present walking cane to plow her way through the pew. She stopped at the end, snatched off a newly placed turkey paper figure, and tore the head off. Despite her proclamation of salvation a few seconds ago, she wasn't about to hide her agitation and that turkey was only an example. When Mother Pray Onn wasn't happy, wasn't nobody happy. She stood with her legs slightly parted, at least in her mind, a few feet away from the reverend. With one hand on her tiny hip, she began to reprimand him with what thus saith Sasha, the false prophet-profiteer.

"I needed to get a little closer to you, Reverend Tom," she began. "I was sitting over there in the nosebleed section of the second pew" — she used her cane to indicate the exact row she meant — "in the first seat on the far end, befitting my position as President of the Mothers Board. So I can't always hear you correctly."

That's how she started. But then she continued with, "You must've lost your doggone mind if you think I'm gonna let you get away with squandering my year's tithe of one hundred and forty dollars and twenty-six cents!

"I'm supposed to just shout on and give the Lord the glory anyhow? I'm supposed to dance a happy dance after you gambled and wasted my hard-earned social security money?"

Reverend Tom flinched as soon as the word gamble left the old woman's mouth. He hated gambling and had preached against it from the day of his installation, and he knew she knew it. Nevertheless, that was not the moment for correction.

"Well, Mother Pray Onn —"

That was about as far as the reverend got when the first sounds of murmuring reached the pulpit floor. He looked toward the altar's side pew but didn't get much support from the Church Board or the Finance Committee. They all turned and looked back at him as though he were brand new.

Mother Pray Onn and her posse of backsliders viciously tore the reverend and his vision apart. There wasn't a spirit left untarnished — holy or otherwise. He left the church wondering if God had ever called him to preach, or had he just shown up and volunteered. An hour after the church service ended he was lucky he still had Jesus on his side.

Later that afternoon, back in his home, the reverend pushed and rammed the iron poker into the hot coals as he stoked the fire in his fireplace. With every thrust, he cringed as he recalled what had gone down earlier.

The vision of the revolt caused him to snatch a bottle of blessed oil off the mantel and anoint his head with handfuls before he walked over and sank back onto his sofa. All he could do at that moment was reread the tattered pages of his Bible. He'd been foolish to rely on either the Church Board or the Financial Committee for support.

Reverend Tom felt he needed to read his Bible. It was his life's puzzle solver. Yet even after reading practically all one hundred and fifty Psalms, he still felt uneasy. Whom could he call when he couldn't get a prayer through? "Certainly not Ghostbusters," he quipped.

Reverend Tom needed his prayer partner and adopted spiritual mother, Sister Betty. Two days ago, she'd left word that she'd gone to Belton, South Carolina to "handle some personal business," and he prayed she'd already returned.

He peeked out the side window to his garage. From there he could see the far side of Sister Betty's house. The lit front porch light told him that she'd not returned. He went back to his den, called her, and left a message that she should contact him no matter what time she got home.

CHAPTER 4

It was well past midnight when the reverend's phone rang. He'd hardly slept a wink but when he saw the number on the caller ID, he immediately woke up.

The reverend yawned and answered. "Hello, Sister Betty."

"I'm sorry to call this late, Pastor," she apologized. "This storm has made everything a mess. My bus ran late from Belton and when I got home, I was too pooped to do anything. I saw that red light flashing on my phone but didn't bother to check it right away because nothing good ever comes out of me doing so."

By the time Sister Betty finished her long apology and explained her adversity to checking her messages, the reverend was fully awake. He'd barely told her about the mess caused at the church by Mother Pray Onn, and his reaction to it, when Sister Betty started to whip him with the Word.

She gave him scriptural uppercuts from the Old Testament, and then TKO'd him with scriptures from the New. When she finished he'd apologized more to her than he had to God.

"How is God gonna give you a vision and then not give you the provision?" Sister Betty hissed. "Now I don't mean no further disrespect, but you are acting like you forgot that God gave me that same vision and it was about the same time He trusted you to bring it about." She waited for the reverend to dispute what she said, but he didn't. He couldn't.

"Reverend Tom, now tell me we didn't shout about it in your study when God showed us back then that there wasn't gonna be a need for a mortgage? You can't. And didn't the good Lord say to name it the Promised Land? Now I already told you that I'm tired from this long trip and my body is sore. I ain't got time to feed you Bible Similac like you a new babe in Christ. You're the head of the church, and if the head don't believe, then why would the body?"

Sister Betty went on to say a lot more as he held the receiver away from his ear. She captured his guilt when she mentioned that the body wouldn't believe if the head didn't.

When he placed the receiver back against his ear, he heard her say, "If your faith ain't increased by tomorrow when I go down to that bank then don't come with me. I may have a ton of money in that bank but I can't blackmail them with haters and faith blockers in my way."

The next morning, Reverend Tom was exhausted. Sister Betty's telephone rebuke had pushed sleep aside and given him a lot to ponder.

However, despite her rebuke, on Monday morning he couldn't help but remember his history with her. As he read the morning paper, the thought of her brought a surprised smile to his face.

Sister Betty was one of his most senior members and had been a blessing to him ever since he took over as pastor. Her quirkiness was well known to some and a puzzle to most. As far as he was concerned, she was a woman who had God's ear. He had also adopted her as his spiritual mother, especially since both of his parents passed away long before he had finished college, and she was always telling him what to do anyhow.

She also watched his back. The desires of several unmarried females at the church had looked to add the title of First Lady to their letterhead and bank accounts. Moreover and sadly, there were also a few married women who would have made an exception to their marriage vows, had he given them a reason.

Through the good and the bad, Sister Betty had never left his side. She made certain he knew that God had not left either.

Before he knew it, it was around noon and time to pick up Sister Betty.

As he drove out of his driveway, Reverend Tom whispered an affirmation. "God in heaven, forgive me for my unbelief and my unmerited pride in what you've placed in my hands. But Lord, all days are your days, too. Now, if Moses didn't let the Red Sea stop him from helping his people, I'm not about to let the threat of a lack of current finances or a congregation of unbelievers stop me from helping mine."

Reverend Tom slowly pulled into the winding driveway of Sister Betty's luxurious home. Before he could step from the car, she stepped outside to meet him.

She was dressed in her traditional all white everything. She'd bundled up so tight she looked like a white box with a large Bible attached to its side. She stayed ready for any storm — natural or spiritual.

Sister Betty's small feet hopscotched

through the puddles until she made her way inside the car. Without ceremony or waiting for him to open the door, she said, "Praise the Lord, Pastor."

"Sister Betty," the reverend replied. He chose to leave it at that.

She chuckled. While fastening her seatbelt and giving him the once over, she said slowly, "You look like you are still holding onto about a quart of faith so I sure hope you're ready to roll for the Lord this glorious day."

Judging from the way that she acted at that moment, it was hard to believe she'd just chewed him out the night before. Nevertheless, the joy only lasted long enough for him to put the car in DRIVE. Before they'd gotten off the block she became more like a Mama Betty than the Sister Betty he needed.

She adjusted the scarf around her neck and pointed to the car heater. "It's so cold in here I can see my breath. Now turn that thing up. I told you I don't have hot flashes no more and I need a lot of heat."

Reverend Tom did as she requested. He then waited a moment until she adjusted to the blast of heat before he added, "Okay, my short but powerful Ride or Die gal. Let's go and reclaim the Promised Land."

"I don't know how many times I need to remind you that I really don't like the word *die* used in the same sentence as my name," Sister Betty murmured.

"Don't worry about that." The reverend laughed as he finally pulled out of the slow-moving traffic. "You are not going anywhere anytime soon. Heaven doesn't need you up there as much as I do down here."

"From your lips to God's ears and His will." Sister Betty sat back. Her head leaned to the side as she thought, *I want to thank you Lord for Your grace and for Your mercy, too.* A smile crept across her face as she praised her God.

Much to the reverend's surprise, he looked over and smiled, too. "I see you're smiling," he said softly. "Are you and God collaborating again?" He let out a laugh when he saw the surprised look upon her face.

"Why yes, Reverend Tom, we are constantly in cahoots."

"Mind sharing what God has revealed?"

"It's not so much what He's revealed to me as much as me discussing with Him where we're going to end up."

"Oh, I see. You mean the Promised Land."

Sister Betty shifted her Bible and winked. "That's right, me and the Lord are chatting about the Promised Land. So now you quit interruptin' before I have to start speaking in tongues to keep you out of my heavenly business."

The reverend returned her wink with a smile and turned up the heat just a little more in the car. "Well, Sister Betty, I'll get us to the bank and see about the Promised Land in about ten minutes instead of forty years."

CHAPTER 5

Another twenty minutes passed and the Reverend Tom and Sister Betty were still on Highway 29 chatting about everything and nothing. It was raining hard and the driving was slow and cautious.

As they continued to forge their way, they approached a huge billboard set off a little way from the highway.

"Oh my," Sister Betty craned her neck to see through the downpour and the rapidly moving windshield wipers. "It looks like somebody won the South Carolina Mega Lottery. Our schools can use the assistance. It's about a hundred and sumpthin' million win from what I can tell."

"Saying it's for the schools is just an excuse to have folks gamble away their hard-earned money," the reverend said sharply. "God doesn't approve of gambling. The Bible says not to throw your pearls after swine."

"But God . . ."

The subject lit the reverend's hot button and he refused to let Sister Betty sway him when it came to that subject. "There are no *buts*," he said. "Imagine if I took the church's money and spent it on lottery tickets to help get us out of this fix?"

Sister Betty felt she'd chew a hole in her bottom lip to keep from saying her piece. She turned away and continued to look out the window as she thought, *Why not? You wouldn't be the only one or the first at Crossing Over who does.* Even she'd bought a raffle ticket a time or two at the senior center. In fact, she'd won a savings bond and a floral centerpiece.

Reverend Tom and Sister Betty continued to drive in silence for the rest of the way. Neither would sway the other and at that moment, they faced issues that were more important.

"Just look at God," Reverend Leotis Tom said as he strummed his fingers along the edge of the steering wheel. He slowed down the car and lowered his window. He became excited as they passed the Crossing Over Sanctuary church.

"Everybody in and around Pelzer knows Crossing Over Sanctuary is a blessed church. Hallelujah, we don't owe a dime on

46

those six acres where it sits. Mortgage-free is the way to be," he boasted as he pointed along its perimeter.

"God's showing me that despite our current lack of finances and with half the tithes-paying congregation gone, He's still in the blessing business. By this Christmas, His promise will be fulfilled and we'll be blessed with ten more mortgage-free acres right across from where we worship now."

"I'll hallelujah to that and you can raise the heat," Sister Betty replied through her chattering false teeth. "The vision God gave to you to purchase and build on those ten acres will bring a lot of good to a lot of folk. I'm proud of you for following God's lead. It's a big responsibility for a young pastor."

The Reverend Leotis Tom ignored his shivering and smiled, nodding his head in agreement. "Never had I imagined, at the age of thirty-three when I started pastoring, that God would show so much favor."

"Yes, indeed. That's what I was trying to remind you about last night when you were talking all crazy like somebody with no faith." Sister Betty chuckled. "But I guess if God used David when he was a kid to slay a giant" — she shifted her Bible in her lap — "I guess even with the smell of Similac baby Christian milk still on your pastoring breath, He can use you, too.

"Okay, I know you're excited . . ." Her lips fluttered from the cold and that made it hard to keep her false teeth from falling out. She couldn't even finish the sentence before he butted in.

The reverend shivered just slightly, but it wasn't from the cold. He blurted, "Sister Betty, isn't it wonderful to just feel the presence of the Lord all over this land?"

Sister Betty nodded her head in agreement, then murmured, "I'd like to feel Him, but I'm frozen." She would have said something more but her teeth and lips seemed frozen.

The reverend finally rolled up the window with the image of Crossing Over Sanctuary fading behind them. He turned toward Sister Betty and confessed, "I haven't told you everything."

"Oh really . . ." she whispered.

"Yes, I'm afraid I wasn't as forthcoming as I should've been. When it appeared yesterday that anarchy would topple the church and me, well, I didn't bother to finish spreading the bad news to the congregation."

"Let me guess," Sister Betty replied through clenched teeth that'd finally warmed a little. "No one in the congregation knows we have until Christmas for a miracle to happen."

"No ma'am, they don't."

"And of course, you know that I know there's something else you haven't told me either. I always know when you're trying to spare my nerves."

He didn't question how she'd known. As usual, she'd trumped him. At that moment, how she knew and what she knew didn't matter. She knew.

Warmed up enough to allow her frozen lips to part Sister Betty turned toward the reverend. "Now listen, son . . ."

She called him son. That meant despite everything that had gone down in the past ten minutes, she was about to nail his butt to the wall. Of course, she'd do it respectfully. After all, he was still her pastor.

"Stop acting like I don't know that the payments on the Promised Land are almost three months late," she said sternly.

She watched his face cringe and tried to soften her rebuke. "At least Crossing Over ain't got a mortgage to worry about and its taxes are up to date." She reached over and tapped him on his shoulder. The move caused him to jerk around and face her. "I'm proud that you've stepped up to the plate and that you've been secretly return-

49

ing half your salary back into the church's bank account."

Reverend Tom's jaw gaped. He was about to explain why he'd not shared that part with her, but she quickly shifted her Bible again, and pointed it toward him.

"I ain't blind either. I can see even with all the fundraisers and soul revivals we've held that more folks are leaving the Crossing Over Sanctuary, and even quicker during the past year and a half."

The reverend should've felt relieved that he wouldn't have to continue to carry the burden and keep it from her. Nonetheless, when he saw her push her cap and her wig along with it to the side without shame, he knew she was just winding up.

"Even if I am blessed with enough money to carry me through in comfort, I know that the country is in a crisis. There ain't a day gone by that I don't find out that a lot of people here and about have lost jobs, and to a degree, have lost their faith. Of course, when that happens tithes got to fall off."

The Reverend didn't need rocket science to tell him that somebody on the Finance Committee had talked too much or Sister Betty was more of an insider with heaven then he'd known. One thing was for certain, he'd continue to listen and show respect so he could find out who the leak at the church was. It wasn't as if she was going to shut up before she'd had her say, anyway.

The reverend continued to hold his peace, waiting for Sister Betty to pause and let him say his piece. "I've been thinking about one fundraiser in particular," she said slowly. "I know I was against it in the very beginning because I could see nothing good coming out of it."

When Sister Betty was deep in advisory mode using political correctness to keep things in perspective she often closed her eyes. It made her appear a bit more thoughtful. It also caused her not to see the smile that began to spread across the reverend's face. It hadn't taken but a few more minutes before she'd provided the opening.

"Every time Bea and Sasha get together with a plan, folks around them come close to backsliding. This time I think they may be on to something." Sister Betty shuddered suddenly. She thought perhaps that it had gotten colder. "I like this idea of a Seniors Prom right here in Pelzer, right after the Thanksgiving holiday. I attended the one held in Belton a few months ago and it was just wonderful. Whenever I talk about it to seniors I know, they all start reminiscing and everything . . ."

"Oh really." Reverend Tom took a hand from the steering wheel and laid it across the back of her seat. He was about to say more, but decided to let Sister Betty open that door just a little wider.

"Oh, they just love it. In fact, I've heard that many of the seniors from other churches who went to the one in Belton are coming to this one, too. I've already discussed it with my old friend, former Congresswoman Cheyenne Bigelow. Many folks don't know that she's the one who helped put the one in Belton together."

"I don't believe I know a Miss Cheyenne Bigelow." As soon as he said that, he stopped. He liked the planning side of Sister Betty and didn't want to stop the flow.

"I didn't expect you to know her because you're anti-political except when it comes to our first half-black president. That's okay with me 'cause I like the handsome fella and his beautiful family. But 'cause she's had a very colorful personal and political life, Cheyenne Bigelow keeps a low profile, so you don't need to bring up her name, in case you're thinking about doing so."

Sister Betty let her words linger for a moment and when he said nothing more, she continued. "If it's a success, then other churches will want to take turns having it on a yearly basis." She grinned like a giddy young schoolgirl. She liked the idea that her pastor hadn't interrupted again and let her have her say; not that she'd expected different from him. "It probably won't be in time or make enough to help our current fiscal mess, but it's still a good idea."

The reverend's smile couldn't get much wider without his lips meeting somewhere in the back of his head. That's when the smile slid from Sister Betty's face and her right knee twitched. And the pain, she was certain, didn't come from the coldness.

Sister Betty never stood a chance. The reverend had already made up his mind. "I'm placing you on the board with Bea and Sasha."

He saw the look of civil disobedience flash upon Sister Betty's face but he would not budge. "I need you to keep them in line. You did such a great job in Las Vegas. . . ."

Sister Betty's heart raced, and if she hadn't been strapped in that car seat, she'd have fallen over. *Oh Lord, my sins have found me out. Why didn't I just tell him everything that happened in Las Vegas? I almost backslid when Bea and Sasha dragged me into the casino in Las Vegas. I gambled . . . I won money and I liked it for a moment.*

She hadn't told anyone about what really

happened once she'd returned from the Annual Mothers Board meeting. She'd done a miserable job of babysitting Bea and Sasha. Plus, she didn't want the teasing that would come from the members. Sister Betty returned from Vegas feeling they stood a better chance of forgiveness from him if he thought they'd done a little prostituting instead of casino worshipping.

"That's a load off my mind." The reverend continued smiling. If he'd sensed a change other than her usual rebellion, he didn't respond.

Just as Sister Betty's tongue was about to launch into her many excuses, the reverend's cell phone rang.

"Hello." He clutched the phone to his ear as his head shook from side to side as though that action alone would negate what he heard. "What are they doing at the bank? You tell them I'm coming down there!" The reverend seemed not to care that he was screaming into his phone. "You tell them that for me!" He slammed down the cover on his phone, disconnecting the call.

"Sometimes they make you want to snatch off your collar and grab a pistol!"

The reference to a pistol caused Sister Betty to flinch. "Do you want to tell me what's going on?"

The reverend's hands were almost bluish from clamping down on the steering wheel, but his face was turning red from the anger. "The Devil is at the bank with demons in abundance." He drove off with the wheels of the car screaming through the rain.

CHAPTER 6

How Reverend Tom managed to get him
and Sister Betty to the Piece of Savings
bank in less than twenty minutes was anyone's guess. His car looked as if it had had
a mud bath when he careened into the parking lot. He and Sister Betty didn't look
much better.

"My Lord Jesus, I didn't think we'd make
it without the police chasing us here." Sister
Betty stood shaking like a wind-up toy and
she kept tossing her Bible from one hand to
her other. "Next time, I believe I'll walk the
ten miles."

Once they entered the bank, neither
Reverend Tom nor Sister Betty was surprised to see a few members of Crossing
Over Sanctuary. The dismal economy played
the great equalizer in the lives of many of
the church members. They were in dire
need of financial assistance. He'd done as
much as the church's budget allowed for

several families and it still wasn't nearly enough.

Reverend Tom and Sister Betty made their way into the bank's outer lobby where they ran across more of their congregation, who'd ventured out in the storm seeking assistance. When he saw their defeated looks, it reminded the reverend of his purpose and the vision God gave him.

He felt his muscles and his jaw tighten. His mission was indeed critical and he quickly returned to the problem at hand. Lucifer had thrown a monkey wrench into the plan. However, Reverend Tom believed that between their prayers, he and Sister Betty were enough to turn that monkey wrench into a boomerang.

"You wait for me out here in the reception area," the reverend told Sister Betty. "It shouldn't take too long to see if they've changed their minds."

"I still don't see why you think they would." She looked to her pastor for an explanation. He hadn't fully explained why they'd rushed when they were going there anyway.

As much as he needed to hurry, he gave her the short and edited version of the urgent phone call. "BS — Bea and Sasha — visited the bank a little while ago. Apparently, they left before we arrived because I don't see nor hear them about."

"Bea and Sasha came to the bank?" Sister Betty gave a questioning look. "Why would they come here?"

"Yesterday, during the morning service, Mother Sasha accused me of embezzlement. She said I misused her one hundred forty dollars and twenty-six cents tithe and offering. It was the full amount she gave for the entire year."

"Say what!"

"Oh hold on. It gets better. Apparently, she came here to order the bank to audit the church's accounts and find out what happened to her money."

"And why did Bea come?"

"BS always follows one another." The reverend shook his head and straightened his minister's collar. It was a reminder of who he was in God's plan, because at that moment, he could've become a criminal.

It took Sister Betty a moment to comprehend what her pastor told her. She clasped her hands together and her eyes silently pled when she asked, "Do I still need to work with them? I'm not in the best of health. Those two would kill me. You know how I feel about dying just yet. . . ."

Reverend Tom pivoted and walked away

without responding. He could only handle one crisis at a time. Sister Betty's would have to wait.

About fifteen miles away from The Promised Land development and five miles away from the Piece of Savings Bank sat one of Pelzer's long time restaurant eyesores, The Soul Food Shanty on Ptomaine Avenue.

The building, with its second floor of illegal efficiency apartments, had survived twenty-five years. It had more health violations and pest exterminations than any law allowed. Yet the local police and health department employees, along with several misfits, ate side by side. The only things separating them were huge bottles of Pepto Bismol and bottles of Hell Naw Hot Sauce.

Because the Thanksgiving and Christmas holidays were approaching, the Soul Food Shanty hung its usual mismatched holiday decorations. The owner kept it simple. There was one large cherub holding the horn of plenty purchased years ago from a craft show. It was made of felt and covered a hole in the wall by the kitchen. That was the Soul Food Shanty's contribution to the holiday spirit.

Despite the Shanty's lack of style and ambience, it offered privacy if one didn't mind the noise from the kitchen. Seated at a table for one was Crossing Over Sanctuary's member Trustee Freddie Noel.

Fifteen years ago, he'd arrived from Harlem, New York, with nothing more than a thank you Jesus for Your grace and mercy, and forty dollars. That same day, he moved into one of the Soul Food Shanty's upstairs rooms, and downstairs was where he ate every day.

Back in Harlem, he'd spent most of his adult life working as a janitor for a large department store that never paid much. So, as bad as times were, he knew a thing or two about stretching fifteen cents into a dollar.

At one time, financially, things looked like they'd change for him after he'd had an accident that involved a huge bus. The accident was reported in all the newspapers and on television. The company's drunken bus driver sideswiped the trustee's car, totaling the car and the trustee. He'd spent months in full body traction and when it was removed, he still walked around with one arm bent at the elbow and one leg bent at the knee like a dancing robot on a Soul Train line. Finally, through prayer and physical therapy Trustee Noel regained a semblance of a walk, although he still gal-

60

loped when he ran.

He'd sued the bus company almost five years ago for reckless endangerment and won. The bus company appealed immediately and hadn't stopped appealing since. Most folks long ago dismissed any notion that the payout he'd won against a big bus company plagued with worrisome appeals would ever happen. As far as his church was concerned, he would remain broke and ugly. And it certainly made it easy to understand why Bea chose him to hang coats at the upcoming Seniors Prom.

That morning, just as every morning, Trustee Noel sat down to eat alone. As usual, when he ate he always ordered whatever was calorie-laden in the hope of gaining weight. He alternated between a platter of pig's feet fajitas, turnip greens with jalapeno peppers, sweet tea, and buttery pound cake for breakfast, lunch, and dinner. Of course, his taste in foods were as left-to-center as his looks and he remained reed thin.

He had no appetite. What he did have, however, was something that weeks ago had changed his life forever, but he'd refused to believe until he saw it for himself.

"Are you having coffee this cold morning or iced tea?" The question came from Chef

Porky LaPierre, the short, dark, and squatty owner of the Soul Food Shanty. He stood blinking his one good eye that made him look like a human traffic light. He also held a large dented tin can with puffs of smoke struggling to escape from whatever was in it that passed for coffee. "And I can't keep reheating those pigs feet until you decide to eat while you take up space in my establishment."

"Just sit the pot right here." Trustee Noel pointed to an uncluttered spot on the small round table. "Don't worry about the rest of the order. I'll take it with me."

"You can take it wherever you want to, but you ain't taking it upstairs to your room. You know I don't allow no eating in your room. It costs extra for the exterminator if he has to climb stairs." Without saying a word Chef Porky turned around, returning to whatever concoction he'd been creating before.

Freddie Noel never touched his coffee. He stretched and tried to alleviate some of the back pain he'd felt since he woke from sleeping on that lumpy bed mattress. Having gotten as comfortable as he could, he looked again at the letter he'd quickly brushed aside when Chef Porky appeared. He didn't need the man in his business. Yet

62

if Freddie had read the letter once, he'd read it one hundred times since he received it weeks ago. His skinny hand swept slowly across the letter's official logo.

The South Carolina State Lottery congratulates you on being the sole validated winner of ONE HUNDRED AND TWENTY-FIVE MILLION dollars. Because you've elected to have a one time pay out, your net winnings amount to SIXTY-FIVE MILLION DOLLARS. Enclosed please find your check in the amount of same . . .

His hands shook. In his mind, the rustling sound of paper was certain to bring attention his way so he quickly dropped the lottery notice back onto the table. Freddie reached up and began to twirl a small and thinning silver sprig of hair. He looked almost childish as calmness slowly spread over him and a grin surfaced. The only thing he didn't do, at that moment, was suck his thumb. Instead, he leaned back in his chair and tried to suppress a smile.

CHAPTER 7

An hour had passed since the Reverend asked Sister Betty to wait and, instead, he was the one who waited. He did so at the behest of the bank's owners. He sat inside one of the huge bank offices where all he did was pray, and count ceiling tiles.

While the reverend fidgeted and fretted waiting on the bankers, Sister Betty remained in the outer reception area, and pulled out her spray canister of holy oil. If it went down badly inside for the pastor, she had her finger on the trigger. She'd douse any demon in the vicinity.

They were almost an hour and a half late, but finally, the owners of the bank filed through the door. "We hope you haven't waited too long." The insincere concern came from the one of the Cheater brothers named Skimp. "How are you? We haven't seen one another since the church contracted the land you've designated as the

Promised Land."

The *we* in question that almost caused the reverend to backslide on the spot were the albino Cheater brothers, Skimp, Slump, and Ted. They were billionaire triplets and owners of the bank.

"Please follow us to our office," the second Cheater brother, Slump, said as he got in lockstep with his brothers.

The main office of the Cheater brothers had dark oak wood-paneled walls and thick black carpeting that came up to the ankle. Crystal chandeliers hung every few feet, and floor-to-ceiling palms graced each corner. In the middle of the monstrosity of a room stood a huge, glass-encased carving of a Mississippi riverboat. Reverend Tom couldn't speak. He'd never seen such opulence and could've forgiven them for all their slights when he saw the walls adorned with Renoirs alongside famous Louisiana artists R. C. Davis and William Hemmerling.

In unison, the Cheater brothers, with their pinkish-red skin hanging beneath their chins like a turkey's wattle, leaned back in their chairs and took ugly to another level. They knew they were ugly, but it didn't matter. They were number two on the Filthy Rich Billionaire list.

However, time was money and so for the first time the unified Cheater brothers showed emotion. They rolled their chairs closer and one of them spoke the name many feared: Mother Sasha Pray Onn.

The atmosphere turned toxic and almost freezing cold at the same time. It was as though they were all in church and Sasha had just walked in and taken her place on the Mothers pew.

Slump's beady eyes suddenly turned into orbs of anger. He began twisting in a chair that looked as if it would topple from his weight. "That woman had the audacity to accuse our upstanding and fine reputation as bankers of swindling, as well as aiding and abetting your church!"

Ted Cheater interrupted and almost broke out in hives as he recalled Sasha's outburst. "And then she pounced upon the customer service representative and scared that poor woman to death as she demanded an audit for her one hundred forty dollars and twenty-six cents tithe."

He swelled with anger, "She can't play a playa! We ain't rolling wit that!" His puffy pink hands flew immediately to his mouth. He glanced quickly at his brothers and back at the reverend. No doubt, he was shocked that his first billion dollars hadn't com-

66

pletely erased his New Orleans gangster tendencies or hidden his appreciation for the rich rappers.

Skimp Cheater couldn't speak. He'd punked out already from the moment they'd mentioned Sasha's name.

It became the reverend's turn for temporary amusement. What they were upset with Sasha about was nothing new. She kept folks upset about one thing or another.

From that moment on, the reverend tried to take advantage of what he saw as the brothers' weakened condition. However, every time he tried to turn the conversation around to the community's need for the Promised Land development, the Cheater brothers rebuffed him.

Finally, Reverend Tom had enough. "The Devil is a liar!" His eyes blazed, and his lips curled with anger as he blurted out the familiar exorcism.

None of those three human turkeys moved.

And that's when the palm of one of the reverend's hands hit the arm of the chair, sounding as though a whip had cut the air. He was so angry even his complexion seemed to change as though his face was a kaleidoscope, red to brown and back to red again. "Y'all think I'm supposed to just sit and wait until y'all get good and ready to discuss your unfairness? My God won't tolerate doing his anointed harm."

Reverend Tom cut the histrionics when he saw they still appeared united as one unmovable and unsympathetic unit. He decided to try another tactic. He took a deep breath. "I'm sorry." The apology was insincere, but necessary at that moment. "It is just that this development comes as a total surprise. Please allow me to explain in a more Christian-like fashion."

He leaned with his palms on the table and stared at the men. "I come to you now, as a man of God, just as I did three years ago. I humbly ask you to reconsider and give the church at least a six month extension before you exercise the option to use a forty-five-day notice to call in the loan. We are a church trying to do God's work for the community. The community's monies keep this bank solvent. Moreover, you only stand to gain if we complete the building project."

Seeing the resignation on the reverend's face finally provoked the Cheater brothers to move. One by one they leaned across the table and laid the thick files down in front of the reverend. Looking from one to the other without saying a word, they waited a moment or two before they nodded together in agreement.

Skimp Cheater was the first to speak. "We've heard everything you said."

Slump Cheater tapped his brother on the wrist to keep him from going further. He leaned forward and clasped his hands while peering over glasses that somehow slid down and rested upon the tip of his beak-like nose. "Just like you, Reverend Thumb —"

"It's Reverend Tom."

"Okay," Slump said softly. "Didn't mean to mispronounce your name, Reverend Tom Thumb. I, too, believe in a higher being and huge depositors."

As if on cue, Ted Cheater interrupted and blurted, "It's almost two o'clock. It's time to seek that higher being and another huge depositor." He quickly leaned over in his seat and grabbed the nearby remote control before he continued. "Our answer," Ted's voice rose, "to put it quite bluntly, Reverend, is *no!*"

With their response given, the three Cheaters turned toward a wall-mounted television and turned up the volume loud enough to dispel any demons left from their meeting, along with the Reverend Tom. They sat on the edge of their seats. They listened and watched as the financial commentator frantically tossed papers onto the floor, then a second later a bell clanged in homage to their personal god.

"Please leave," Skimp ordered when he noticed the reverend had not yet budged. "I'm sure when you want to confer with your God, you too, like privacy. We require the same with our higher being, the Wall Street Stock Market."

"Oh, by the way," Ted added. "To show we're not totally heartless, since Christmas is on a Saturday this year and we'll be closed —"

"We'll give you until Monday, the twenty-seventh," Slump said quickly. "Have a Merry Thanksgiving and a Happy Christmas or a pleasant Felicidades or whatever. We know we will."

Even through the heavy oak door, which he slammed as hard as he could, Reverend Tom heard the three turkey trolls snickering. His burden was now so heavy he could hardly lift his head. He could not believe God had allowed this to happen.

He walked back into the waiting area where he found Sister Betty still waiting. She had her hands clasped in prayer and hadn't looked up yet. He let out a loud cough to catch her attention. "I'm sorry I kept you waiting."

"It's not a problem," Sister Betty replied as she struggled to stand on her stiff legs. "I've been praying and I believe I may have a way to quash Bea and Sasha's craziness."

At first, the reverend didn't answer. At that moment, he was still too livid and disappointed at how he'd represented God.

"Did you hear me, son?"

Reverend Tom looked at Sister Betty and tried to bring a smile to his face. "I'm sorry. What is your plan?"

"I'll tell you, but I want you to release me from baby-sitting those two."

"What is your plan?" Reverend Tom repeated. He really wasn't in a compromising mood.

Sister Betty peered into his eyes and saw a defeated man looking back. She decided to revisit the deal later. "I've already put it into place, but we need to make a stop on the way back."

"Sister Betty." Reverend Tom's shoulders seemed to disappear from weariness into his coat as they walked to the car. "I'm so tired. I'd rather just drop you off wherever you need to be and I'll just go home."

"Okay, I understand. On the way, if you just drop me off at the Shanty, I'll call for a ride home."

Reverend Tom's eyes met hers. She had

him and they both knew it. There was no way he'd ever drop her off at the Shanty in that part of town and let her catch a ride home.

By the time, they left the bank it was Life: 10 and the Reverend: 0.

CHAPTER 8

As soon as they arrived at the Soul Food Shanty, the rain tapered off. The reverend checked his watch. It was almost three o'clock and he'd accomplished nothing, yet he was hungry.

"You look famished," Sister Betty said as though she read his mind. "Do you want to get something to eat inside while I'm here?"

"At the Soul Food Shanty?" The reverend's disdain for the place showed as his clapped his hands and sneered. "I don't fancy mystery meat and Alka Seltzer at the moment."

Sister Betty pulled a handful of Now and Later candy squares from her coat pocket. "Here," she offered. "Eat some now, and save some for later."

Finally the reverend laughed. "Never mind, I'm not much for candy. Why don't I drive on down the way and pick up something from a legitimate fast-food place. Can

I get you something?"

Sister Betty quickly rattled off a list of what she wanted to eat. She chuckled, then quickly dismissed the reverend's reminder that she'd tried to poison him with the Shanty's food.

Inside the Shanty, Sister Betty found Porky at the cash register. They'd not seen each other in a while so they took a moment to catch up.

Having no success at getting the latest church gossip that he savored, Chef Porky pointed to the back of the room to where she could find Trustee Noel.

"Good afternoon, Trustee Noel." Sister Betty smiled and motioned for Freddie to remain seated when he tried to stand. She dragged a chair from a nearby table and removed her coat and hat before she sat and placed them in her lap. "I was so surprised to get the telephone call from you."

"It's good to see you, Sister Betty." Freddie took her coat, and belongings. He dragged another empty chair over and laid them across its back.

"I still don't know how you knew I was at the bank when you called."

"I didn't know," Freddie explained. "I called about another matter and the receptionist mentioned that you and the pastor

74

were there. I wanted to talk to you anyway, so I figured I'd just reach out to you while I could."

"Well, did you have another dream or something?"

Sister Betty was good at interpreting dreams and he'd questioned her often. She figured he'd had a very exciting one when he insisted she come by.

It took a few minutes for Freddie to get to the point. Two seconds after he told her about the lottery winnings, Sister Betty's wig almost few off. Freddie then handed her the envelope from the South Carolina State Lottery Department as his proof.

"It's because of how you interpreted that dream and the vision I last had. I did exactly as you told me to do on that piece of paper you handed me after Prophet Kay Pow breathed on me."

Sister Betty started clawing at the torn tablecloth. She searched her mind from the forehead to the back of her neck and couldn't remember telling him to gamble.

"What did I write?" she said. "Refresh my memory."

"I can do better than that." Freddie grinned. "I still got that piece of paper in my pocket. I've been carrying it around ever since you handed it to me."

75

He pulled the faded small slip of paper from his pocket and handed it to Sister Betty. The first thing she noticed after changing her glasses twice was that it wasn't her handwriting, but then she turned it over. On the far corner of the paper, she saw it.

"Oh, my Lord, Trustee," Sister Betty whispered. "This is all a mistake."

"How can millions of dollars be a mistake?" Freddie thought perhaps Sister Betty had lost her mojo with that crazy talk.

"Listen, Trustee Noel." She looked around to make sure no one was within earshot before she spoke again. "Earlier in the service that Sunday, I needed something to write down the weekly assessment levied on my Missionary Board dues for our upcoming anniversary next May. I usually pay my dues once a year, but I'd forgotten and needed the breakdown."

Freddie leaned in closer. Confusion was hitting him harder than a stick on a piñata. "What does that hafta do with the millions I won?"

"I'm trying to tell you," Sister Betty snapped. "I'm sorry. Let me get to the point. I always keep a pad of paper in my Bible to jot things down on, but it wasn't there. Bea was sitting next to me so I asked if she had a piece of paper I could write on. She fished around in her pocket and handed me a piece of paper. I never paid attention to the writing already on it."

"But why give this to me if it wasn't because of the dream I'd told you about that week?" Freddie began twirling his sprig. He wondered if Sister Betty wanted a piece of his action and that's why she was weirding out on him. But she had money and never seemed that type of Christian. He was more confused than ever.

"Trustee Noel," Sister Betty began. Her wig was almost laying completely to the side of her head exposing tiny gray cornrows. She didn't care and didn't try to straighten the wig. "Who collects the assessment and dues monies for the auxiliaries?"

The light bulb turned on in the trustee's mind and he shot forward in his seat. His hands landed on top of Sister Betty's hands. "I do," he whispered. "Me and sometimes Brother Leon Casanova."

"Well Trustee, that particular Sunday it was you. I gave the paper with my assessment *and Bea's gambling budget* to you. You were supposed to write it down in your book so you could match it with the check whenever I gave it to you."

"Y'all okay over here?" Porky arrived

without making a sound despite his three hundred pounds that normally shook the room. "Y'all look like ya got ya heads together about something. What's goin' on? Y'all know I like to hear the news, too."

"Well, why don't you come to church more often?" Sister Betty said as she pushed the slip of paper under her pocketbook on the table. "That way, you can hear it first hand and it won't be called gossip."

Anybody but Porky would've been insulted or gotten the hint. But Porky didn't get hints and, even less often, tips. "C'mon Sister Betty, you know I do my worshipping on Sundays on Saint Recliner."

Chef Porky turned around almost toppling tables as he laughed his way back to the cash register.

Sister Betty pulled the paper from beneath her pocketbook. She scanned it closer and looked up just in time to see Freddie almost pulling out the last few strands of his sprig.

She began reading from it. "2 Scratch Offs, 2 Lucky 7s, and 2 Set 4 Lifes." She removed her glasses and asked, "Did you buy all the ones written on this paper?"

"I did, except I added one of my own."

"You did? What was it?"

"I purchased a one dollar Mega Lottery

ticket and had the machine select the numbers."

"Well, I guess the right thing to do is give Bea her part of those scratch offs. How much did you win from them?"

"Nothing."

"You mean to tell me the only ticket that was a winner was the Mega one?"

"Yes."

"Well, let's hope that Bea don't remember what was on that paper, although I don't see how she would know I gave that paper to you."

Then Freddie threw water on her theory and told Sister Betty how on the day he'd purchased the tickets he'd run into Bea and Sasha. "I'd already bought the tickets when they walked in so I didn't even check the lottery ticket or the scratch offs. I didn't want them all up in my business so I stuffed the tickets in my pocket and scurried out of there. Once I found out I'd won, I went to Anderson to collect and told the publicity people not to say anything. I don't want my face splashed all over the place."

"So now you're sitting on top of sixty-five million dollars and nobody besides the Lottery folks know but me and you?"

"Well, the Piece of Savings Bank knows about it. That's where I put my money."

"But that's the bank that's putting the squeeze on the church."

"I know," Freddie said. "I need your help to put the squeeze back on them. I've never had this much money before. I can help save the Promised Land if you promise to help me."

"Oh Lord, I'm getting a headache from all this. I'm not in the best of health, you know, and I'm not ready to die yet . . ."

Freddie dismissed Sister Betty's angst. He'd not finished giving her some more. "But this is not why I wanted to see you."

Sister Betty leaned back in her chair, so caught up in the history of that tiny sheet of paper she'd forgotten he hadn't revealed everything to her. "Well, the pastor is coming back to pick me up, so you'd better say so while we're alone."

But Freddie never got a chance to tell Sister Betty all he'd had to say. Reverend Tom had entered and headed their way.

"You just keep your mouth shut until we can chat again. Meanwhile, stay clear of Bea and Sasha unless you *have to* deal with them."

Sister Betty had rushed through her instructions so fast all the trustee heard was "shut your mouth."

Trustee Noel did just as she'd told him.

80

He didn't speak, even when the pastor reached their table and said hello.

CHAPTER 9

"I know Trustee Noel can be a bit eccentric, but he was just downright rude." The reverend and Sister Betty were in the car. He'd been complaining about the trustee ever since he'd informed her that the fast-food places in that area were subpar. He'd refused to buy anything, and was still hungry. He couldn't eat, but he could fuss. And so he did. "How could that man just sit there and twirl his top hair instead of saying hello?"

"He's had a rough day." That was all Sister Betty could think to say. "I guess it's been tough for a lot of us today."

"Well, it's about to get tougher," Reverend Tom declared. He drove as though he'd caught a second wind. Without explanation, he drove past the exit for their street and headed toward Crossing Over Sanctuary. His lead foot pushed the speed limit.

Despite her need to keep her mouth shut

and remain upright, Sister Betty could feel the impatient shift in her pastor's demeanor. It did not sit well with her at all. "I see we're headed to the church. By the way, do you want me to drive?" she asked cautiously.

"Sister Betty" — the reverend's voice dropped an octave lower, sounding like a growl — "you don't know how to drive."

"I know that," she snapped, "but at this moment, I'd certainly feel a lot safer if I were driving than having you behind the wheel of the car."

"You're right. I'm sorry." Reverend Tom eased his foot off the accelerator. "Brother Casanova called me on my cell while I was trying to find something to eat."

"And that made you want to drive this car like a rocket ship through the rain?"

"No." He peered over at her, then winked. "I just need to meet him at the church and it will only take a moment."

"So what is it you're not telling me?" Sister Betty allowed a bit more indignation to lace her words than necessary.

"No more than what you're not telling me. I have that third eye, too. And you're up to something."

She sank back into her seat just in time to see the huge billboard on the side of the highway. WE HAVE A ONE HUNDRED AND

She needed God in a hurry. "Step on it! Why are you driving so slowly?"

Severe thunderstorm threat or not, Sasha and Bea called a meeting for that afternoon. They needed to tidy up the details of the Seniors Prom. Thanksgiving was less than three weeks away and no one had reported progress or hindrances. Of course, neither woman cared that assignments weren't even a week old.

Sasha had to make a tough choice, putting a temporary halt to returning to the bank. It was necessary that she put aside her anger about her pastor mishandling her tithe for the good of the Seniors Prom.

Bea, on the other hand, wanted to ask around a bit. She'd let Sasha trick her into cutting a fool earlier at the bank. It wasn't going to happen twice. At least not in one day, it wouldn't. She'd started to reassess things lately, because her moneymaking schemes weren't paying as they once had. For much of Bea's senior years, life seldom varied. She levied spiritual assassinations on her enemies through whispered prayers. Her survival on a meager social security check was rivaled only by her passion for bingo. Moreover, it didn't mean she wasn't concerned when folks chuckled about the money she spent buying cat food for the cat she didn't own. She had a taste for tuna . . . and sometimes the money ran out too soon.

Once the old mothers arrived at the church, they immediately went downstairs to the fellowship hall. Just as the women expected, Elder Batty Brick and Brother Leon Casanova sat waiting for them.

The seniors gave halfhearted greetings. They said a quick prayer and prepared for business. Elder Batty Brick checked his watch for the third time and asked, "Where is Trustee Noel? Why isn't he here?"

"He didn't need to be," Sasha quipped. "He don't need a plan to hang up no coats, so let's move on."

Once Sasha explained it that way, they all agreed and continued the meeting.

"I might as well get this off my chest." Sasha took off her glasses and quickly dropped, then raised her head. The move made that gray bun on her head look like a ball bobbing in a fishpond.

"When the pastor said the church done gone broke," Sasha said, "it almost broke my salvation, too. How is that man gonna promise to take us to the Promised Land, and then break that promise?"

Brother Casanova and Elder Batty Brick

pulled their chairs closer together. Since they sat on the Finance Committee, they already knew they were in her sights. Fortunately, they'd already made a pact that unless they were tortured with pitchforks they wouldn't reveal the Christmas deadline.

"Ah ha . . ." Elder Batty replied slowly. He then crossed his arms as though he'd not attended that past Sunday's service and heard the announcement.

Sasha narrowed her eyes and with her cane, she reached over and tapped him on his bad corn by accident. When he jumped in his chair and jerked his foot back, she made it seem like she'd done it on purpose. "If you don't want me to pop that corn I'm gonna need more than that from you. I want an accounting of my one hundred forty dollars and twenty-six cents!"

Leave it to Brother Casanova not to have his hearing aid turned all the way up. When he misspoke, he truly misspoke. "Mother Pray Onn, the last thing we need is for one of our dearest tithe payers to feel put upon. We're already looking into the situation and you'll be happy with the results."

Bea, who'd actually tuned Sasha out, wouldn't believe anything Brother Casanova said. As she'd often said, game recognized bull crap. "He's lying. Everybody knows

86

Sasha ain't never happy. Sasha won't even let nobody write *Happy* on a birthday cake."

"I beg to differ," Brother Casanova snapped. "I'm a changed man. I don't hafta lie."

Bea's arched back already had her almost on top of the man. It wasn't hard to intimidate him when she ordered, "Gimme a quarter!"

"Well, er . . . I'm afraid I don't have change." Brother Casanova cringed and watched Elder Batty slide his chair away. Brother Casanova had stepped into Bea's trap so fast, he'd gotten egg all over his face and his cheap hearing aid.

Bea had shot down Sasha's petty gripe and Brother Casanova's change-even-he-didn't-believe-in. She needed the meeting back on track and addressed her concerns.

"We need to get the important matters out of the way," Bea said as she shifted her big butt around on the small chair. No matter which way she moved, that butt spilled over both sides of the chair.

"Brother Casanova" — Bea pulled a pad and a pen from her pocketbook — "I'll keep the records. Ya supposed to get the decorations. Did ya get anything?"

Brother Casanova, still annoyed with Bea, adjusted his hearing aid to its lowest setting. Even if she hadn't called him out, he'd still adjust the hearing aid. Bea's rough voice always gave him an earache.

"Well, seeing how it's been only a few days, I haven't gotten a lot of materials. However, I did ask Reverend Tom's permission to use whatever was available from the drama department. I'll know better once he gives me the keys and I look the things over."

"Ya just make sure ya get enough mistletoe," Bea huffed. "Ain't no sense in having no prom if we ain't got no mistletoe."

Up to that moment, Sasha hadn't offered any new ideas. She hadn't quite figured out how she would repay Bea for interrupting her tirade earlier, but she would. In the meantime, she didn't like Bea taking over the meeting and wasted no time hurling an insult. "Why are you worried about mistletoe, Bea?" Sasha snapped. "Ain't nobody paying top dollar to kiss She-Rilla!"

Bea leaned forward and growled, "Don'tcha worry about it 'cause when it's over, ya can just kiss my —"

"Mother Blister," Elder Brick interrupted with his hands outstretched, "Please!"

"Please this," Bea said as she rose. She wiggled her backside and passed the gas she'd held in all day. "I've got to go to the bathroom. There ain't quite as much crap in there as there is out here."

Bea's big hips hadn't quite cleared the doorway leading to the hallway bathroom before the other three started gagging.

That noxious odor made Sasha weep and she kept stabbing at the air with her cane as if it would protect her from the smell demons. Poor Brother Casanova's nose twitched like a rabbit. He almost ripped his ear off trying to adjust his hearing aid to keep the smell from entering.

But old Elder Batty Brick caught it the worst. He reached into his jacket pocket and withdrew an old tissue that dropped like a rock into his lap. He tried to grip it but it was so full of holes it looked like a hive without the bees. He crammed it up his nose so hard his finger was stuck.

It took another five minutes or so before the three inhaled enough clean oxygen to keep their brain cells alive.

When they'd revived and Bea still hadn't returned from the bathroom, Sasha's anger had escalated to the point where she didn't care how she said it as long as she said it. "In all my years of playing church, I ain't never witnessed such a mess. Why would that heffa stand here in this hallowed place before the *omnipotential* God and fart?"

89

"I'm with you on that one," Brother Casanova shot back. "I don't even wanna see a sample of the T-shirts she's working on. I'm through and my head hurts."

He whined so much Sasha was inclined to give the man a hug. But Sasha didn't do hugs unless she meant it as a stab in the back. "Let's just move on."

With that said, they agreed not to wait on Bea. Elder Batty Brick spoke. "Now, I've collected about $3750.00." He did a quick count using all his fingers and his two knees, and still got it wrong. "At twenty-five dollars apiece, I've sold two hundred tickets."

Somehow, the figure didn't seem right to Sasha and Brother Casanova. The way they quickly glanced at each other signaled they wondered if he'd slipped back into his bad habit of embezzling. But since neither finished high school and had failed arithmetic, they said nothing.

By the time Bea returned, they'd accepted Elder Brick's money report without one challenge. Brother Casanova's combined DJ playlist with a mixed tape of the Platters and Tupac caused no concerns. And Sasha, although she hadn't yet secured a caterer, had managed to blackmail enough seniors into participating in the date auction. And they still didn't want to see Bea's T-shirt sample.

Bea returned in a better mood. A lot of what had her angry in the first place she'd left in the bathroom. "What'd I miss?"

"A doggone manners class, that's what you missed!" Sasha hissed as the two men helped her to her feet.

Sasha left Bea standing in the middle of the floor with her mouth wide open. Of course, Sasha couldn't leave Bea like that. She stopped and pulled her arm out of Brother Casanova's, turned back toward Bea and hissed, "You old Sasquatch."

Now Sasha felt free to leave.

CHAPTER 10

By the time Reverend Tom and Sister Betty finally arrived at the church, Brother Casanova had left. Neither the reverend nor Sister Betty knew about the meeting Bea and Sasha had held, so Bea gave them an update on the Seniors Prom.

Believing every word Bea said had the reverend almost shouting. "So there's going to be a packed hall and your committee has everything in order. I just love it!"

Sister Betty watched Bea telling her version of the truth. Sister Betty's knee had jumped with just about every word that flew out of Bea's mouth. That meant Bea was either delusional or lying. The odds were fifty-fifty either way.

"So you see," Bea concluded, "when we sell off the T-shirts and auction off the dates, that's gonna bring a lot more money to the church." Her face lit up. She didn't need to lean on Sasha for support. She could stretch the truth on her own.

Sister Betty decided she'd stay silent. Perhaps the reverend would forget about tossing her into the mix since he believed Bea and Sasha had it under control. Of course, she wouldn't have to go forward with any crazy plans to get Bea and Sasha out of her way. Every BS problem seemed as if it would resolve itself.

Reverend Tom offered to drop Bea off at her home. Although she lived in the opposite direction, he wasn't finished with his interrogation by a long shot. The ride would give him more time and with her stuffed in the backseat alongside a praying Sister Betty, Bea was apt to be more truthful.

By the time the reverend pulled up in front of Bea's building, she'd given up the skinny on the gambling habits of Sasha, three of the Mothers Board members, and about twenty other church members that gathered weekly at bingo. The only thing Bea didn't give up, according to her, was sex.

"But we still manage to pay our tithes no matter how little or how much we win," Bea gushed.

"Mother Blister, how long have I preached against gambling?" Reverend Tom had to bite his lower lip to keep from jumping in the backseat. "If I am to believe all that you've told me, I've taken in gambling money as tithes, too?"

"It bought the robe ya wore at Brother Chauncey's funeral last year," Bea replied. "Ya looked real handsome in it, too."

She continued to reveal how many of the members held everything from backroom pool championships to running bets on who betted the most for the week. The football, basketball, and baseball seasons' gambling tithes kept the electricity paid at the church. "The most money we've made on a weekly basis comes from who can name the mystery meat served at Porky's on Thursday nights."

Reverend Tom gripped the steering wheel so tight his pecan brown skin turned walnut black. He struggled to remain civil and pastor-like as he asked, "And why haven't I known about all this gambling going on right under my nose all these years?"

Bea didn't answer her pastor because she hadn't finished telling it all yet. She folded her fat arms and ran down the list of folks who didn't attend the church that often, but gambled and also paid tithes to keep the church going.

Sister Betty turned to Bea to signal her not to say another word but Bea liked being the pastor's pet for the moment. Sister Betty couldn't have stopped Bea with a bullet to the heart.

"To answer yo other question" — Bea beamed — "ya wasn't supposed to know, that's why ya didn't. Ain't ya the one always preaching about how to keep stuff in season and out? Well, knowing about gambling ain't in your season. The congregation knows how high fallutin' ya is, but we still love and admire ya for it."

She leaned back and winked at Sister Betty who'd sunk back farther into the car seat. Bea didn't care. She was so proud she could've thumped the hump out of her own back.

Reverend Tom felt like a fool after learning about all the stuff going on in his church and right under his nose. He'd been so busy preaching about what they shouldn't do that he'd not paid attention to what they did do. "The Devil is a liar!"

It was the second time in one day the reverend felt like cussing. He couldn't and he wouldn't, but he could sacrifice Sister Betty and he did.

"Mother Blister," the reverend said as calmly as possible, "I appreciate you and the Mothers Board, along with all the members of the church, but I fear we must revisit a few of our tenets."

"I didn't know you visited tenants, Pastor. I thought you just went around praying for the sick and shut-in folk from our church." Bea beamed. At that moment, she was truly proud of her pastor and his unselfishness.

Reverend Tom almost ground his teeth down to the roots trying to remain civil. "I meant tenets as in some of the laws and rules that govern our church." He shook his head and made up his mind to just do it and not discuss it.

"I've decided to have Sister Betty work with your committee. She's an alternate member of the Church Board and you need a board member overseeing the prom." He threw it out there the same way he'd have said, "Have a nice day."

Before Bea could protest, Sister Betty spoke on both their behalfs. "I told you, I'm not well. I'm an old woman and I don't wanna die before my time."

Bea exited the car without a word. Once she got inside the door she took off her coat, raced to the phone, and dialed Sasha's number. When Sasha didn't answer, she left a message. **"Sasha, this ain't the time to act like ya still mad at me. We got a bigger problem 'cause Reverend Tom done throw Sister Betty on our Seniors Prom Planning Committee!"**

It wasn't an hour later that Sasha arrived at Bea's apartment. As soon as she'd entered her living room and heard Bea's message about Sister Betty, she grabbed her hat, her cane, and called for a ride.

Over the years, Sasha and Bea had embraced the old adage the enemy of my enemy is my friend when it came down to Sister Betty's interference in their business.

No quicker had Bea let Sasha through the door, than she started. "Look at this clap trap you live in." Sasha pointed to the mismatched green, purple, and orange kitchen chairs that had *flea market and yard sale* invisibly written on them.

"Listen up, Thumbelina. I didn't call ya to listen to ya mess. We'd better get Sister Betty off this committee. Ya know she's too holy-fied to work with us."

At the mention of Sister Betty's name, Sasha's anger surfaced and reminded her why she'd rushed over. She threw her cane in the corner of Bea's living room and nearly decapitated one of Bea's fake potted palms. "You are right. We can insult each other any time. So what do you think we should do? Reverend Tom can be mighty hardheaded once he's made up his mind about some things."

"We'd better hurry and think of somethin'. Thanksgiving is in two weeks and soon after is the Seniors Prom. I hafta finish up these T-shirts so it's gonna be up to ya to get rid of her."

"Other than killing her I don't know what we can do." Sasha let the thought linger just in case Bea wasn't totally against harming Sister Betty.

"Naw, we can't kill her," Bea answered as she tried to tape the big leaf back onto the palm. "I've already been to jail. Ya would be somebody's appetizer and I wouldn't last past supper."

With Sister Betty thrown on board the Seniors Prom sinking ship, they actually took time to ask God for permission to slay His right-hand gal. They also remembered to ask God to do something about the recession. Neither could afford their costly medications for their varied physical and mental needs.

And that wasn't good for them, the church, or the country.

CHAPTER 11

The next week sped by. On the Sunday morning before Thanksgiving, Trustee Noel arrived at Sister Betty's home as planned. They had been calling each other regularly since their meeting at the Shanty two weeks ago.

"Come on in, Trustee Noel." Sister Betty led the shy man into the living room and offered him a seat.

"Thank you," Trustee Noel said as his skinny body sank and almost disappeared into the overstuffed pillow at his back. "You have a lovely home."

"I'm glad you like it." Sister Betty noticed he wore what looked like something new. She wanted to say something but didn't want him to feel overwhelmed by kindness. "Can I offer you something to drink?"

Trustee Noel shook his head. He was nervous and needed at least one hand to twist that hair spritz on the top of his head.

When they'd chatted earlier in the week, they decided that although the trustee had the bank check for twenty-five million dollars, they doubted the reverend would change his position on what he'd called ill-gotten gains.

"He'd be a fool to turn down this check." Trustee Noel had argued that point repeatedly. Once Sister Betty told him the bank had turned down the request for an extension twice, he became more adamant. "I'm on the Finance Committee. The bank is not playing. They don't lose."

"I know," Sister Betty replied. "The way the bankers see things, if the church loses the Promised Land, they get the land back, the structures, and the money from whoever purchases it. If the church uses your money, then the bank cashes the check, and they still have your money."

"There's got to be a way we can put the squeeze on the bank and the pastor. If we can, the church doesn't lose the land or its leader. The bank will go after the reverend for certain if the loan isn't paid."

"Well, we'd better come up with something," Sister Betty said as she pulled her coat from the closet. The trustee rose and helped her with it. "Thanksgiving is next week and so is the Seniors Prom. Time is moving and we'd better be, too."

When they reached Crossing Over Sanctuary the parking lot was almost empty. The worshippers who did attend trudged inside without smiling. It hardly mattered, because the ushers rarely smiled anyway.

Trustee Noel escorted Sister Betty to her regular seat behind Bea and Sasha. It'd been her assignment for years to sit there and spiritually handcuff them with prayer. If she weren't vigilant enough or even went to the bathroom during the service those two old women broke loose and ignored every church rule and protocol before the offering was raised. Sister Betty saw Sasha was seated, but Bea was nowhere in sight. Tha wasn't a good sign. Sister Betty was gla she hadn't shared her plan to get rid them by paying them off. She was m certain than ever the reverend would have gone along with it, but she still di want any part of their planning commi

As she looked around the empty se the sanctuary, she felt a sadness that smothered her. "My Sweet Lord prayed. "You can't let Your people the wayside like this. Lord, show to do."

Placing her Bible on the pew b she folded her hands. The choir

101

number, sang the songs of Zion as best they could. A few minutes later, those in the sanctuary stood, the weight of their individual situations etched on their faces. The heavy doors from the prayer room creaked as they slowly opened, signaling the pastor would emerge. Immediately the congregation opened their Bibles — their swords as they called them — and began to sing, *"Welcome into the place, welcome into this Sanctuary . . ."*

Reverend Tom chose a deep purple long-sleeved robe with white and gold trim blazed along the hem and along the zipper line. He'd always referred to it as his fighting gear. The purple represented the Royal Priesthood that he took so seriously. The robe came to him as a gift from the Pastor's Aid Society. According to Bea the Pastor's Aid had sold raffles right there on the church grounds.

His eyes swept his congregation as he adjusted the heavy gold cross around his neck. He laid the small notebook that held his "thus saith Lord" sermon on the pulpit, feeling like a fraud, unworthy to lift the spirits of those who needed so much and had so little.

The truth was that the reverend did everything he could to avoid preaching that morning. Precious sleep had avoided him last night. The energetic light that normally shone in his brown eyes had faded and he felt as though his soul had suffered a black-out.

"Take your burdens to the Lord in prayer." His soul wept and no one saw the tears. But he hadn't done that. His burden remained embedded because he'd refused to accept that he wasn't the Super Pastor. His head dropped and he laid a hand against one ear as he often did when the preaching got good. Not this time. His hand laid across his ear because he grappled with the sound bites Bea had pushed into his head.

He motioned for the choir to sing another song. He felt he needed more time to gain composure. He looked over at the Mothers Board. He saw Sasha, but couldn't find Bea as he scanned the congregation. Where was she? Had she thrown a stone and hidden her hand?

He couldn't get past it. Yesterday, in a fifteen-minute car ride, the old church mother, with her quirky outlook on life, and her customized church devotion, had yanked the covers off. She had managed to unveil not only his church members' flawed worship, but his as well.

Somehow, at the very moment, the choir

sang *"I come to the garden alone"* and the congregation waited for a word from the Lord, Reverend Tom thought of Moses, who fell from favor and was not permitted to lead his people to the Promise Land. Would the same fate await him?

CHAPTER 12

The morning service was well into its second part and the collection plate was near empty. No one had cut a step for the Lord and it felt more like a funeral than a hallelujah good time.

Reverend Tom summoned the courage to preach despite his need for rest and a firm rededication to his God. The message he prayed about and edited from a previous one while he waited in his study received a lukewarm reception.

Several times while he preached "Time to Make a Change," he heard someone say aloud, "You need to change." In his entire time preaching before his congregation, he'd never felt so low.

Reverend Tom slowly came to the realization that truly broke-in-the-pocket folk would break the rules. The members had gone from calling out "amen!" to heckling the man of God.

While the reverend struggled through the service, Trustee Noel struggled, too. He sat with his hands folded across his skinny chest and glared. He wanted to cry out, "I've got the millions we need to get us to the Promised Land!", but he couldn't. His bullheaded pastor's stand on gambling stood in the way. The only thing moving during the uninspired service were the hands on the clock . . . and they moved slowly.

While trustee Noel pondered what to do so did Sister Betty. She prayed, wept, and did everything but rush up to the pulpit and shake her pastor by his thick neck.

Then the sound of low murmurs broke out over the sanctuary and Sister Betty's head jerked toward the source. She saw him; she knew it was him because it looked like a silver streak of lightning flashed through the front pews.

Before the trustee reached the podium to join the reverend, Sister Betty's knee buckled. It jerked as though a rubber band held it and then broke. It shook enough to cause it to fall away from its resting place on the back of the pew in front of her where it waited to trip Bea, who'd finally arrived, and Sasha before they could cut up again.

"Praise the Lord, Pastor." Trustee Noel called out. He became almost out of breath as he wrestled with one overzealous usher who tried to stop him.

The trustee held up his white envelope and waved it to get the reverend's attention. "Pastor, please I have a special announcement." With one strong jerk, he completely threw off the usher twice his size.

From the moment her pastor walked to the pulpit, Sister Betty began to feel uneasy. It grew worse, once he waved away another usher who'd rushed to join the first one holding the trustee.

"Come on, Trustee Noel" — the reverend beckoned — "say what's on your mind. God wants our all when we worship."

"I wanna save my church," Trustee Noel blurted. He made a final run and it looked as though he tackled the reverend before he thrust the envelope into Reverend Tom's outstretched hand.

Although the reverend's body and spirit felt spent, he managed to remain upright. The skinny trustee actually felt like a gnat had landed upon him.

Meanwhile Elder Batty Brick who sat not far from the trustee remained frozen. The only part of his body that moved was his head and neck, which he managed to swing toward Brother Casanova.

Elder Batty Brick had said nothing, but

Brother Casanova didn't need to turn up his hearing aid when he saw Elder Batty Brick mouth the words, *Number two pencil has snapped.* Brother Casanova nodded his assent. They thought the same thing. No matter what Bea and Sasha said, there was no way they were going to trust that crazy man to hang up the coats at the Seniors Prom.

It didn't matter at that moment what others thought. Trustee Noel was riding high. He literally galloped in on those bad feet and was about to save his church.

He was dressed in what he believed was the latest in Super Saint apparel. He wore one of his new JCPenney suits that were Buy One Get Three. He knew he was dapper sharp.

The chocolate brown suit with matching brown leather shoes held the reflection from an overhead light and it made him feel handsome. He smoothed a wrinkle in his light blue shirt and straightened his brown and blue tie. With a dramatic finger gesture, he made certain everyone saw the huge fake cubic zirconium pinky ring, and motioned to the reverend to open the envelope. When he'd dressed that morning he'd promised himself to act blessed and not shy.

His eyes darted about the congregation,

looking for Sister Betty. He hoped she'd show a sign that even though he'd not stuck to the plan, he had done the right thing.

When his eyes finally met hers he saw a woman who seemed to levitate off her seat in anger. She glared at him and shook her head. He saw her fumble with her Bible and shift in her seat. None of it was a sign of encouragement, but it didn't matter. Reverend Tom had opened the envelope.

By the time the pastor held up the bank check and laid his arm on the trustee's shoulder, Sister Betty's knee had almost jerked out of its socket. "Oh heavenly Father," she moaned.

Her head dropped to her chest. The trustee had jumped the gun and she knew nothing good was about to happen. She prayed, "Bind that Devil right now."

No sooner had Sasha and Bea overheard Sister Betty pray to ask God to bind the Devil, than each sat up in their seats. Sister Betty might not have wanted to see drama, but those two old drama queens started salivating.

While the entire congregation sat stunned or waited for an impromptu Jerry Springer moment, Reverend Tom adjusted the microphone so he could address the church. Unaware that Sister Betty, back in her seat, prayed on his behalf, he felt light as a feather.

"I have in my hand manna from Heaven. This is God's answer to fervent prayer and the key to our Promised Land." Reverend Tom stopped to let the congregation absorb his words while he clutched the trustee a little closer with one massive arm.

"This is a check for twenty-five million dollars." Reverend Tom barely spoke the words, before the church's playful organist started playing a remix of Johnny Kemp's hit, "Just Got Paid."

A quick glaring rebuke from the reverend brought that unscripted part of the service to a halt. The shameless organist sank back into the organ bench.

One of the ushers who stood near the last pew overheard the pastor's announcement from the back row where for the entire second part of the service, he'd stood resting on one of the seats instead of at attention or handing out fans.

He leaned in and whispered to a seat-filler seated on the edge, "I betcha that trustee must've finally gotten that big money from that lawsuit."

That's all it took. Within a few seconds, any of the nasty comments ever spoken about the trustee flip-flopped and somersaulted. As the rumor went around the sanctuary, folk started squirming in their seats as if the Spirit had touched them. If the church were on Facebook, Trustee Noel would've reached his friend limit within the first five minutes.

With the check secured in his hands the reverend felt sufficiently rebuked by his own conscience. He did have favor with God. He'd never been in danger of losing his reputation for getting things done in the community, and he held the proof.

He was happy enough to want to plant a kiss on the trustee's cheek. However, in keeping with his macho man image, he shunned that feeling and hugged the trustee, instead.

"Trustee Noel," the reverend began, "I am in shock! But I'm certainly not surprised. What a mighty God we serve that He would show out like this." Reverend Tom's arms pulled the trustee closer and they shoulder bumped.

Trustee Noel's physique was not built for chest or shoulder bumping. He could feel the bruise forming on his skin. "Ow. Suh."

"That's right, praise Him in tongues!" Reverend Tom encouraged. "Give Him glory in tongues!"

Trustee Noel began to shake. The pain of

the shoulder bump set off tremors in his body. He knew one thing. He would use some of those millions and join a gym.

When it appeared the Spirit or whatever had finally subsided, Reverend Tom addressed the trustee again. "I know you've got something you'd like to say before I begin to tell you how grateful the entire church and community is because of you."

Trustee Noel spoke slowly and painfully into the microphone. "Thank you, Pastor. My heart is too full to say a lot more, but this church is my home."

Reverend Tom accepted the quick words of appreciation, then added a few more of his own. "Crossing Over Sanctuary church cannot thank you enough. I know it must come from somewhere deep in a giving heart for you to give so much."

The reverend stopped and for reasons only he could explain, he raised the trustee's hand and added slowly, "You have millions of dollars, more than enough money from your insurance award. You've adhered to the principle of sowing and tithing as the nineteenth chapter of Numbers instructs us to do. If this is one-tenth of your insurance award . . ."

Trustee Noel only heard the words, *insurance* and *award.* Everything beyond those two words sounded like white noise. He had no idea what the pastor meant, especially since he was still waiting to hear from his attorneys about that particular money issue and the appeals.

If the reverend saw the puzzled look upon the trustee's face, he ignored it. He was overjoyed and continued talking. "I am going to recommend that one of the buildings on the Promised Land be named in your honor."

"Hallelujah! Amen and glory be to God," Sasha suddenly screamed out. It made no sense to waste a perfectly good opportunity to plant a seed of appreciation in the situation. It might sprout into something useful when she bragged about how supportive she was of the trustee from the beginning. In her mind, she'd already assigned the coat hanging duty to Elder Batty Brick.

Ignoring Sasha's over-the-top outburst, Reverend Tom kept on talking and used every word to increase the trustee's stature within the church. By that time, the reverend realized why he'd delivered the sermon "Time to Make a Change." Things certainly had changed for the better. He believed God used Trustee Noel as a Bible-based example of obedience and faith. He saw the gift in his hands also proved he was right about having a vision from God. It'd all come right back to him and his stubborn pride.

Reverend Tom stopped and looked toward the ceiling. He smiled, believing he was listening to the Spirit before nodding his head as though he agreed with it. "Thank you, Heavenly Father," the reverend said loudly. "The Blessed Spirit reminded me that we didn't have to rely on shortchanging our salvation by begging the bank for more time. We can look the Devil straight in his evil eye and tell him God provides. None of us had to *gamble* on our faith."

He turned and winked at the trustee as he continued to speak. "Just look at my God in His awesomeness," the reverend boasted again. "Holy Ghost, lay witness to the truth!"

The microphone in the reverend's hand magically appeared in front of the trustee's lips. Trustee Noel became nervous. His hands started shaking and his lips began to flutter.

Of course, that's when the church and the reverend thought the trustee was about to speak in tongues, again.

Speaking in tongues twice meant no lie could cross the Trustee's lips or he'd drop dead just like Ananias and his lying wife did in the Bible when they lied to the disciple Peter.

Trustee Noel went full into panic mode. He began to sweat. All of his good thoughts about how the reverend wouldn't care where the money truly came from as long as it came, fled. He needed the comfort of twirling that sprig of hair of his, but he couldn't do that, either.

"I thank you Reverend Tom for yo' confidence in me." Trustee Noel's voice continued to shake as he tried to smile toward the reverend.

It's that bank check, the reverend thought as he smiled back at the trustee. *That's what has my confidence.* "Continue, Trustee Noel, and tell what saith the Lord," he said aloud.

It was then or never if the trustee was to tell the entire truth. "Well, you see, uh . . . Pastor, I didn't get my insurance money yet. I'm the one done hit that big Mega Lottery."

If the reverend wasn't so caught up in the moment boasting about what God did and the Devil didn't do, he would've stopped the trustee right then. But the reverend's mind and spirit were elsewhere.

The truth was, while his body stayed at the Crossing Over Sanctuary with the rest of the congregation, the reverend's spirit hadn't. It had already hopped in his praise-mobile and stood proudly in line at the bank. In his mind, he saw himself about to hand the teller the check when the trustee's words jerked him back to reality.

The reverend's pride collided with the truth, and he wanted to wring the trustee's neck.

He threw the envelope back in the trustee's shocked face. "God don't need nor does He want your tainted and ill-gotten money!" Without giving a benediction or waiting for the organist to play, the reverend fled the sanctuary.

Embarrassment wasn't new to the trustee. A day didn't go by that someone didn't rain down shame on him. But this was his pastor, his leader, his spiritual advisor, and the man who, only moments before, had patted him on the back. Reverend Tom had called down God's anointing and blessings. And then that same pastor turned around and slapped him with a paper envelope. Trustee Noel couldn't say a word. He stood with egg on his face and twenty-five million dollars in his pocket.

It wasn't hard to figure out the church members didn't agree with their pastor, and they showed it.

The members started bouncing around in their seats. Like popcorn, they jumped off their pews all over the sanctuary. Some beat their chests and even raised fists toward the ceiling. They wailed, "Why, Lord, why?"

Not all the congregation wept. Instead they buzzed their complaints like a hoard of bees.

"Well ain't this about a doggone mess," Bea hollered as she leaped from her pew. "That dimwit gambles and wins mo' money than I've ever seen, a drat dang Mega Lottery. He done turned sucker and give it to the church."

Bea's voice began to rise as she clawed at her chest in aggravation and agony. "And our uppity pastor done turned it away."

Without saying another word, Bea let one of her chubby arms drop upon Sasha who'd remained seated. Whether Bea did it accidentally or coincidentally didn't matter. That fat arm fell upon Sasha's head and squashed her bun.

Sasha wanted to yell out from the pain, but didn't. She took her cane and was about to poke Bea in the stomach, but remembered she needed Bea's help in keeping Sister Betty at bay. It seemed she'd have to take that insult and pain for the team and get back at Bea some other time.

Sasha peered up at Bea whose attention was on the rest of the congregation. "If I don't bring down this Sasquatch-looking She-Rilla . . ."

While Bea blasted her discontent and the congregation formed a spiritual lynch party, Sasha began to plan a wedding. Just that quick she determined that she truly loved Trustee Noel. She always had and just didn't know it.

The congregation flew from the pews and started to surround the trustee. Some congratulated him and others shook his hand like it was a slot machine lever. Then two instant baby mamas appeared from the choir loft. Each woman, one about nineteen and the other well into her eighties, swore the sixty-something-year-old number two pencil, Freddie Noel, had stuck them a time or two.

From his office, as he disrobed and prepared to leave, Reverend Tom heard the clamor. It wasn't hard to figure out the sanctuary inmates had taken over. It had gone from praise and shout worship to a shout and rebuke match. The refusal of the money had pinned him to the mat. He'd officially lost control of the service and the message.

CHAPTER 13

Over the next several days, the reverend's phone rang off the hook morning, noon, and night. He refused to answer, preferring the answering machine take the member's wrath.

He left instructions for the church secretary to send e-mails apologizing for his upcoming absence due to a personal, five-day emergency prayer and fast watch. "Whatever Websites are involved I want them all updated to reflect the new information," he'd written, attaching the contact information for various church officials so there'd be no reason at all to reach out to him.

However, folk clamored for the reverend's neck and not those of any church officials.

"No disrespect, Reverend Tom, this here is Deacon Lomax. We've called about a dozen times over the last few days. We figure you ain't just lying on your face stretched out without using at least a telephone. Anyhow, like I said in the previous messages, on behalf of the men's choir and the Deacon Board, we're gonna require a blood and urine sample before we let you back in the pulpit. You done lost your doggone mind! Like I said, no disrespect intended."

Deacon Lomax's message was just a sample of the more than twenty-five he received. After about the twentieth phone call, he stopped playing the messages.

The reverend paced, prayed, and anointed just about everything in his home, including the doorknobs. When he returned to his kitchen, he fell onto one of the kitchen chairs and laid his head on the table. Peace wouldn't come. He lifted his eyes and glanced at his wall calendar.

A bright red circle was drawn around the date, the church's annual Thanksgiving Day dinner for the homeless. "My Lord." He'd almost forgotten that he had to cancel that, too. It was the Mothers Board's turn to host the Thanksgiving Feast. Crossing Over Sanctuary's open door policy to feed those in need on holidays was a long-time tradition. The church hadn't missed a Thanksgiving in almost thirty-two years.

An idea came to mind. He admitted in self-reflection that it had as much to do with keeping his reputation as God's favored son, as it had to do with keeping the church's promises.

"We may not have the monies to do what we've always done," he'd said at a recent community outreach meeting, "but we will do the best we can with what we have in donations." He'd authorized the Missionary Board to gather all it had collected from the local businesses and from the church offerings for Thanksgiving. When added up they could afford to give the packages to only the first fifty families that came to the church. Last Wednesday, more than one hundred and fifty families had stood in line.

He'd watched the line from his study and almost wept. "Lord, I don't want to feed just fifty. I want to feed them all." The reverend's prayer was sincere if not a bit misguided. He could've canceled the Seniors Prom, instead.

Pushing aside the memory of another failure, he went to the window, looked out, and sighed.

"The Seniors Prom will probably fail, too." He couldn't cancel the Seniors Prom. Sasha and Bea promised that if left to their own devices they could triple the amount of money it took to put it on. That was one of the reasons he'd put Sister Betty on watch.

It didn't make sense to make three times the money and spend more than half of it on bail for Bea, Sasha, and anyone unfortunately caught up in one of their crazy schemes. But these were desperate times and in desperation, he'd unleashed the church mothers on the community and prayed they didn't cause a tsunami.

The news of Reverend Tom's self-imposed fast-and-prayer-in-the-desert-with-God exile spread all over Pelzer and the surrounding towns. When folks heard about it they shook their heads with combined pity and admiration. The common opinion was that the reverend had tried to reach the status of a Jesus on Earth and lost his mind. What other reason could explain him turning down twenty-five million dollars?

If anyone asked for an explanation from the church officials, they simply replied, "We all fall down, but we get up. He's lying before the Lord so he can get his mind right."

Of course, no one really wanted to ask Sister Betty for information. She became all out of sorts from the moment she'd started babysitting Bea and Sasha. There wasn't a day gone by that she didn't want to hurt Bea and Sasha. They kept her in constant repent-mode.

Sister Betty's angst was real. Bea and Sasha wasted no time in taking advantage of their pastor's absence. BS went into overdrive. They were seasoned troublemakers. Yet those old biddies still needed their precious time to brew a concoction of mayhem. They didn't have time to fool around with Sister Betty in a Christian manner. Sasha and Bea did everything they could to keep Sister Betty out of the loop. They gave her the wrong time for a meeting, but she showed up on time. They swapped her orange-flavored Tang with a Metamucil laxative and Bea drank it by mistake.

Sister Betty managed to show up at every meeting, except the last one, the day before Thanksgiving. She informed them that an emergency came up and she needed to run over to Belton and take care of some business.

Bea and Sasha finally shared with Elder Batty Brick and Brother Casanova their concerns about the Seniors Prom and its prominence.

"We ain't got time to be all fancy, but we don't wanna come across as tacky, either," Sasha conspired. "That's why we gonna reassign what you two need to do."

"I don't see why we hafta come across as tacky, no how," Elder Batty Brick replied. "We got one of the wealthiest men around right here on this committee."

"I already tried calling him, before I called the two of y'all. Do you have cotton for brains?" Sasha hissed. "You think I'd mess with you two amateurs if I didn't hafta."

"Go ahead, Sasha," Bea urged, "tell 'em what that spineless millionaire told ya." Bea stood and pounded her fist, "I swear if I wasn't full of the Lord and interested in writing with that pencil on his checks, I'd have punched him in the mouth."

Of course, it was at yet another meeting that Bea didn't let Sasha get in another word. Bea became so mad she ranted and showered spit all over them. "And then that fool had the gall to try and man-up and tell this fractured Thumbelina" — Bea stopped and flipped the bird at Sasha — "how if his money wasn't good enough for the Promised Land, he certainly wasn't gonna risk more of the pastor's wrath funding no prom!"

Brother Casanova leaned forward in his seat. He adjusted his hearing aid. He'd turned it down as soon as Bea began to speak in that voice he detested. "So he ain't willing to pitch in, is that what I'm hearing?"

"He told Sasha that just because the pastor's a fool, everybody over fifty-five got to suffer, too?" Elder Batty Brick licked his thick lips and started to chew on the bottom one to keep from cussing.

By that time, Sasha's blood pressure had come to a boil and that tight gray bun flipped for real. "Now do you see what you've done Bea. If I'd wanted so much confusion, I wouldn't have told you as much as I did."

Bea's face almost swelled to the size of a basketball. She pointed at Sasha and yelled, "Then ya should've spoken up. We ain't got no time to waste with ya trying to supervise."

"Bea," Sasha hissed, "would you please sit your big butt down so I can tell these fellas what we're gonna do. Save your opinion for the eleven o'clock news."

Bea and Sasha went another couple rounds before Bea got tired of Sasha's reprimands and tried to tie Sasha to a chair using one of her handwritten T-shirts. Sasha's cane came down on Bea's pinky toe and that put a finish to the scuffle.

Of course, none of the group had seen Bea's handiwork before that moment. No sooner had they seen the first word, than Sasha, Elder Batty Brick, and Brother Casanova almost fainted. They kept looking and pointing at the T-shirt but couldn't say a word.

Bea might've been the only one that graduated high school from their group, but it seemed she'd gotten an *F* in spelling and there wasn't a grade low enough for her sense of humor.

She had decided to shake things up a bit for the Seniors Prom. She wasn't happy with the group's suggestions, so she created one of her own. In her mind, she knew what old folk really liked and what they'd do often, if they could. So she improvised her slogan with a cute slant on names of a couple well-known sex pills for men. Every spare moment she had, Bea had worked on those T-shirts.

In bold black letters, she'd written NO VIAGRA — SEE ALICE INSTEAD. Bea had the correct spelling for Viagra, but misspelled Cialis.

It was bad enough that the slogan was inappropriate but the only Alice over fifty who would attend the prom was Alice "Grandma Puddin' " Tart. She was the widow of old Pop Tart, as well as the oldest — age ninety — and most respected member on the Mothers Board. Ever since Grandma Puddin' stopped belly dancing more than forty years ago, she'd been on the grind for the Lord. She'd also been a very active evangelist until she retired and catered dinners every now and again. Bea had resurrected that old woman's dead reputation and maimed her Christian walk with an indelible ink pen on a cheap T-shirt.

Sasha's voice finally returned. "Bea, you old heathen. You went from wanting to kiss under the mistletoe to wanting everyone to use Viagra and sleep with Grandma Puddin'!"

Bea's grin slid slightly. "What y'all know about sex? Y'all ain't had none since it had y'all." Bea turned her hump around to the rest of them and tuned out the disapproval of her handiwork, silent or otherwise. If Bea told the truth, she'd never liked Grandma Puddin' that much no way, so maybe she'd done it on purpose without knowing she had.

Without taking it to a vote, the group silently agreed it was too late to do anything about the XXX-rated T-shirts, but it didn't stop Elder Batty Brick from cupping his hands and bowing his head. He didn't wait on the others to pray. He dialed Heaven immediately. "Lord, please let them not open

127

their welcome packs until they get home."

Once the meeting got back on track, Bea and Sasha explained what they really had planned for the Seniors Prom and that the men shouldn't tell anyone, especially Sister Betty and Trustee Noel.

"We are gonna charge folk for parking scooters," Bea offered. "I wanted to charge them by whether they got a V4 or a V6 engine, but Sasha wouldn't budge from not doing that. We also must have spaces for wheelchairs out in the hallway. We'll line up the canes and the walkers near the back door. We'll charge them to get those back or to use them each time we take them down."

"If we charge ten dollars to park those doggone things it don't much matter what kind of engine, She-Rilla." Sasha's eyes narrowed and she yanked her cane off the floor beside her, shuffling it from hand to hand. She wanted to bust Bea in the mouth with that cane so bad, she could almost taste it. She'd told Bea not to mention that little venture after promising to split whatever they made. Now they'd have to split it four ways because of Bea's big mouth.

Brother Casanova turned the paper he'd written on over to the other side. They'd come up with so many crazy ideas to fleece their paying guests he'd run out of room.

He had put a checkmark next to the ones that were least likely to wind up with them in jail. "So let me see if I've got it all." Turning the dial on his hearing aid so he could hear what he'd written so far, he proceeded to read from the list.

"We're gonna sell single sheets of toilet paper in the ladies room for a quarter a sheet." He stopped and peeked over at Bea and fell out laughing. "Bea better wear one of those coin changers around her waist." He slapped his thigh and bent over laughing, but when he saw Bea rise off her seat, he shut up quickly. Remembering that gas leak she'd deliberately caused at the other meeting, he apologized.

Brother Casanova quickly read off the rest of the get rich quick schemes. "We'll take awful and embarrassing photos and threaten to use them to scandalize folks. We're gonna collect raffle money for the most delusional costume award, too." Brother Casanova continued reading until he'd read enough of Bea and Sasha's crazy schemes to get them all sent to therapy, forget jail.

Elder Batty Brick hadn't said much, but he listened closely. There was a constant look of concern with every item read. Finally, he turned to Sasha for answers. "Sasha, you are the head mother in charge along with your cohort seated over there, but me and Brother Casanova are somewhat respected members of the Finance Committee. How are we supposed to pull all this off and not have fingers pointed or church charges filed?"

Sasha and Bea glanced quickly at each other and fell out laughing. Sasha winked at Bea. "Lord, Bea when you work with amateurs there's so much explaining that's needed."

Bea nodded in agreement. It was all she could do, because laughing always kick-started her bladder, but she was determined to see Sasha set the elder straight.

"First of all," Sasha said as she caught her breath, "we've got a single women church's ministry coming over from the Burning Bushes Center to carry out the dirty deeds. Everyone knows they ain't nothing but undercover gangsters. I promised them we'd rig the bachelor dating auction in their favor and we'd get Trustee Noel to kick in a couple extra bucks."

"You didn't!" Brother Casanova almost yanked out his hearing aide. "You mean to tell me you got Sister Brenda Basket, Sister Tunisia Solo, and whatever gender Cill is claiming lately to run roughshod over people at the prom?"

"That's right," Bea added. "They owe us big time from how we took care of them on that desperate singles' cruise to nowhere they messed up."

"Oh, I like the way y'all think," Elder Batty Brick said, licking his thick lips. "We're gonna make a ton of money that night."

One dumb scheme after another found its way to approval on Brother Casanova's pad. In no time they'd found ways to wreck a perfectly innocent seniors' night and ensure it would be a disaster.

Finally, they said the benediction, satisfied they had the plan to help the church's financial situation. And if Bea didn't run her mouth as much as she ran to the bathroom, they'd put a couple bucks into their pockets, too.

Of course none of them considered the absent members of the group. No doubt when the feathers hit the chicken coop's fan, Trustee Noel and Sister Betty would get egg on their faces, too.

131

CHAPTER 14

Despite all the craziness, whether it was the unseasonably rainy weather or the church in conflict, God gave Thanksgiving a break from both. Because Reverend Tom was out of touch for a while, Sister Betty and Trustee Noel didn't seek his permission to feed a few more of the less fortunate.

They paid Porky to keep the doors open to the Soul Food Shanty and although Porky volunteered to cook, they had the food catered. "It didn't make sense to totally ruin their Thanksgivings," Sister Betty reasoned. "It's just a little something extra besides the turkey giveaway."

While others ate their fill at the Soul Food Shanty, Sister Betty had invited Trustee Noel back to her home. She'd already cooked and decided he could use a good home cooked meal. It also gave them the privacy to discuss how they'd confront Reverend Tom and again try to change his mind about the lottery winnings.

The truth was she'd forgiven the trustee for jumping the gun and igniting that firestorm at the church. Once they started putting their heads together, they really enjoyed one another's company. Thanksgiving Day dinner was just as good an excuse as any other to get together.

There was easy-listening music playing in the background while they relaxed in brown walnut cushioned chairs at a table that sat eight. On the matching brown walnut table lay an orange and brown satin tablecloth. A modest horn of plenty sat on the long fall-patterned runner in the middle, with matching napkins. Sister Betty had never been a big eater and she finished before Trustee Noel, so she sat with her hands folded, and watched him.

He couldn't contain himself. He seemed to forget he could've bought or rented any restaurant he had chosen. When he wasn't twirling that sprig on top of his head, he was lapping at the food like a baby eating its first meal.

He tore into several helpings of roast turkey, sage sausage stuffing, whole berry cranberry sauce, collards, sweet potatoes, and macaroni and cheese. He even finished a quart of diet Coca-Cola with little effort.

133

"I'm not used to feeding someone who appreciates my cooking in such a manner." Sister Betty blushed. "I can't wait to see what you do to that deep dish peach cobbler I made."

Trustee Noel ate that peach cobbler with a ladle and made Sister Betty almost weep with pride. She still had it; she could still cook for a man about her age. That was saying something for a woman who lived alone and didn't date.

Trustee Noel gave his excuses for pigging out and finished belching away the two pounds he gained. "Let me at least clear these dishes away," he insisted. It took him longer than expected because skinny or not, he'd eaten his weight and could hardly move.

A short time later Sister Betty led Trustee Noel into the living room. "You take that Bible I laid out over there and grab a pen and paper," she told him. "We need to pray and ask God for guidance. I know God can show us how to prove to the pastor that blessings have all kinds of roots in their beginnings."

"From your lips," Trustee Noel said softly. "He needs to know that disguised blessings are still blessings."

However, Sister Betty and the trustee

134

weren't the only ones shortcutting Thanks-giving for a talk with the Lord. A few houses over, in his living room, Reverend Leotis Tom did the same, alone.

As others sat and observed the day the best they could, Reverend Tom entered another day of fast and prayer.

For almost a week, he'd remained com-mitted to frequent prayer, and with the exception of liquids, hadn't broken his fast. His handsome face sprouted prickly dark hairs that made him look scraggly. He still had the muscles, but they looked a bit deflated. His signature curly hair was knotty. His body reeked of musk and if air freshener was sprayed in the room, it might've com-busted.

He looked as if he were having seizures. He flipped from praying on his knees one moment to lying prone the next. He couldn't or wouldn't stop nagging God. "Lord, I need You to turn that trustee around from his evil ways."

A self-righteous prayer of complaint about Trustee Noel was all he had to show for his fasting and praying. He hadn't sought answers for his personal failures because he hadn't owned any.

"Heavenly Father, You said not to cast

your pearls before the swine. How can I use that filthy money to build the Promised Land? You said we should not let our good works be evil spoken of." He kept reminding God of God's own words as though God wouldn't remember what He'd said.

Even with all his pleading and fasting, Reverend Tom didn't receive a single word, scripture, or have a vision. "Lord, I feel as though I'm treated like Your disobedient child, and You've placed me on time-out."

He couldn't cry because he'd run out of tears. "How can I be disobedient? I've done nothing but stick to Your word."

It didn't appear that God would answer his prayer so his thoughts turned to Sister Betty. In no other time since he'd started pastoring had he needed his spiritual mother more than that moment. But he couldn't call Sister Betty. He couldn't stand to hear her rebuke because the last one still rung in his ears. *If the head don't believe, then why would the body?*

The phone rang and interrupted his thoughts. Since the reverend hadn't answered his telephone in several days, he wasn't surprised to hear the message, *This mailbox is full. Please call again.* He didn't want to hear the caller's voice or another disrespectful message, so he peeked out his front window and saw the mailbox on his porch was full, too. Some mail had fallen from the box and lay on the wet surface.

Although he was determined not to leave his home until he heard from God, the reverend decided to get his mail. He couldn't leave mail on the wet ground. If the mail carrier became concerned because his mailbox overflowed, the police might come around to check on him. He didn't want to see anyone, not even a concerned cop.

It took him less than five minutes to put on a jacket and bring his mail inside the house. He wasn't going to open any of it, but one stack of mail bound by a single rubber band caught his eye. Written in the lower left hand corner he read the words *forward to* and there was his address.

He sat in his recliner to open the first few on top, then stopped. They were as he suspected — past due notices and other reminders of just how seriously in debt the church had become. He looked at increases in the water bill, the heating bill, and the electric bill. The taxes were paid, but utilities were sacrificed. He could tell from the handwriting on the forwarding notice that they'd all come from the church secretary. He wasn't certain if the Finance Committee or the Church Board were aware of the latest financial woe, and he didn't have time to care. He needed God in a hurry.

Suddenly, he felt lightheaded, and threw the bills to the side. As his head fell forward, in his mind he began seeing angels surrounding him. Whether it was a result of not eating, he didn't know. He felt a strange sense of power return to his body and it sent a stirring in his spirit. He leaped from the chair, fell to the floor, and shut his eyes. A moment ago he'd seen several angels. As he lay, he opened his eyes and saw only one.

The angel had huge muscles such as his and his hair was also dark. He carried a huge purple and red bound book. The angel looked at the reverend, stared hard, then pointed the book at him.

Reverend Tom wasn't afraid. With a free hand, he grabbed at the angel's robe, causing the angel to drop the book upon his head. He didn't flinch, but screamed with authority, "I'm not letting go until you bless me! Tell me what God wants from me!"

Whether he'd fasted too long, prayed too much, or was hit too hard upside the head by the angel's book, it didn't matter. When that stack of past due notices arrived the man of God had gone over the edge.

Reverend Tom believed he was wrestling

with an angel just as Jacob had in the Bible. He kept twisting and turning on the floor. "I'm not letting go. You've got to bless me!" Then he saw that angel swoop down, pick up that book, and commence to whip his behind.

CHAPTER 15

Reverend Tom didn't know how long he'd battled, only that he had.

"Sweet Jesus." He couldn't believe his eyes. His living room looked as though a bomb had destroyed it. As far as he remembered, he'd never left the floor. "Lord, let this be a dream, too."

Another look around the room proved it wasn't a dream. He was awake and cold. The revelation was strong enough to cause him to bolt upright. He pulled his long legs to his chest and rested his head upon his knees. "Lord, what are You trying to tell me, to show me? Please make it plain. I need to understand. I have a headache, too."

He was desperate for answers. That angel had not blessed him, but beat the crap out of him and nearly destroyed his living room.

Reverend Tom shut his eyes, trying to remove the vision of the mess around him and recall the details of the dream. He rocked slightly as he breathed out in little spurts. The chill he'd felt a moment ago no longer bothered him. He rocked and cradled his knees until pieces of the dream slowly returned.

He lay upon a blanket, but he couldn't determine the blanket's material or even its color. Just out of his reach, a large sheet spread before him under a cloudy sky. On the sheet were some of the strangest things. There was a golden castle, and a man dressed in finery stood in its doorway. Like a scanner, a strange white light poured over the man and he handed the castle key and a piece of paper to a man dressed in rags. The raggedy man entered and the finely dressed man walked away.

A huge, opened jewel-crusted treasure chest sat next to a beautiful woman adorned with sapphires, diamonds, and large gold earrings. Around her ankle, she wore a bracelet with jeweled tiny bells, such as the whores in the Old Testament wore. When she walked, the bells rang to let a man know she was for sale. The light that had enveloped the finely dressed man did the same to the woman. Then she dipped into the chest and began handing pieces of its jewelry to an old, deformed woman with unkempt hair. Every time the old woman accepted a piece of the jewelry, she became younger.

Finally, a crowd of people gathered around a young man about his age, dressed in a preacher's robe. Instead of giving something to the crowd, as had the man with the castle and the woman with the fine jewelry, the young man snatched possessions from every- one and the people fell to the ground, moan- ing whenever he touched them.

Reverend Tom jerked free from the recol- lection and threw back his head. It took a moment, but the cluttered living room reminded him that he was at home.

Then he felt a cold wind, as though someone had walked upon his grave. His head slowly swung toward his fireplace. The fire as he'd seen it before had gone com- pletely out, and in more ways than one.

Although he was exhausted, cold, and still somewhat confused Reverend Tom deter- mined that he had to find out what the vi- sion meant. "I know You're finally hearing me, and You're trying to tell me something, Heavenly Father. But what is it?"

He battled again, but it was to get off the floor. When he finally did, he collapsed onto the sofa, not realizing that one of his hands had fallen onto his Bible in its purple and red book jacket until he felt something hard.

Of course, he'd find out whatever God meant in the Bible.

He'd prayed and fasted for a revelation. Now his heart raced, trying to escape the clutches of the truth that may not be a version of what he'd always believed. Not taking the time to light another fire, he thumbed through his Bible.

He started with scriptures that dealt with impure or unclean things. Nothing seemed to touch his spirit until he came across Acts 10:14.

The reverend reread the passage several times, lost in its parallel between the scriptures and his vision. He didn't normally read using a finger to touch every word on the page, but he did just that. He didn't want to miss a word or its meaning.

As he read the verses in the book of Acts he saw that God showed Peter all manner of four-footed animals, reptiles, and birds. Further on he read where Peter argued with God, saying three times, "Not so Lord; for I have never eaten anything that is common or unclean."

The reverend saw that Peter had held the same strong, unshakeable conviction as he had, causing him to rise from the sofa. With the Bible in his hand, he stood by the fireplace and continued to read.

". . . A voice told Peter, do not call impure that which God had made clean."

He slowly closed the Bible, his spirit pricked by the doubled-edged sword's revelation. He thought of Sister Betty and Trustee Noel, how he'd rebuked and embarrassed them. "That was impure, but God made clean."

He started talking aloud as though hearing the words would make the meaning clearer. "It had to start out impure in order for God to make it pure, but does it pertain to everything that's happening now at Crossing Over Sanctuary? How do I know that God's making this particular unclean thing pure?"

After a few minutes of sharing his concerns with the walls of his house, his confusion surfaced again. It was unnecessary and self-inflicted. After all, he'd barraged Heaven with unrelenting questions and when the clear answers came, he balked. In the end, the reverend's stubborn pride handcuffed his mind and the prayer key wouldn't open the lock.

Reverend Tom heard his stomach growl reminding him that it needed more than liquids. He waffled between breaking the all-consuming fast by adding a few crackers to the menu or diving headfirst into a bowl of cereal. The colorful Trix cereal won out.

After eating, he showered and donned a fresh pair of pajamas. He didn't bother to shave because it was late and he wasn't going anywhere. Reverend Tom returned to the living room, rekindled the fire, and hoped he could rekindle his faith, too.

CHAPTER 16

The effects of Thanksgiving on the Pelzer senior citizenry became twofold. Full stomachs and empty pockets put a deep dent in what they'd spend for the Seniors Prom, but they didn't care. Many were born broke and expected to meet St. Peter with an IOU in their hands.

If anyone gave an award for putting on a cheap event, the Seniors Prom would bring home the gold.

Although it wasn't scheduled to start until around eight o'clock, most seniors got a head start on losing their minds. The idea of reliving days gone by put pep in their steps, larceny in their hearts, and additional delusions in their heads.

A THROWBACK SENIORS PROM the flyer read. COME DRESSED THE WAY YOU ONCE WORKED IT.

Sister Betty was the one holdout when it came time to hand out the fliers. She questioned the wisdom of telling seniors to dress how they once worked it. "Most of them can't even find *it*," she warned.

Of course, whatever *it* was didn't matter because *it* was surely a mess at that stage of life. However, there was always more mess to spread.

In all their planning, the things none of the four discussed were transportation for themselves and a fearless escort. Not having to worry about transportation might've set well with Elder Batty Brick and Brother Casanova, but Bea and Sasha weren't going to show up without a prom date. And they had the same plan in mind to solve their dilemma.

Publicly they talked the man down, but secretly Bea and Sasha had each set Trustee Noel in their sights. Neither mentioned to the other any inclination toward dealing with the man. Neither trusted the other to keep away from the embarrassed, but still rich, Trustee Noel. Both were determined to track him down.

Bea found him first. She figured since he'd missed the final meeting he'd want to make sure he had everything prepared to hang coats. She didn't know if he'd made other plans regarding that particular assignment, but it didn't matter. What mattered was that he was downstairs in the fellowship hall.

Bea stood in the doorway, blocking his exit. "Praise His mighty name," she whispered softly, but loud enough to get his attention. "I had no idea when I came by to drop off my box of handwritten T-shirts that ya be here."

Trustee Noel turned around and couldn't believe his eyes. There stood Bea looking at him much like he imagined a female praying mantis would look at her victim. He'd never played football although he enjoyed the game. When he saw Bea blocking the doorway, he couldn't think of one tackle to move her out of bounds that wasn't a foul.

Believing she had control of the situation and him, Bea threw the box of T-shirts onto a nearby table. She hurried and recited her menu of love. Since the prom started in a few hours, she didn't have time to lay all her sexiness out there.

"How are you Bea? I didn't know you were here. I was on my way out and I-I-I . . ." He blubbered like a fool and his hand shot up to his head and yanked on that sprig.

"Now Trustee Noel, I can't speak for some of these other heathen members, but I sho' appreciate how you want to help out the church."

148

Bea's legs widened as she stood in the hall's doorway hoping to block him from leaving. "I'm taking it upon myself to show you just how much the Mothers Board loves and appreciates all that you're gonna do. After you take me to the prom," Bea said running her tongue over her thick purple lips, "I want ya to come back to my home. Waiting for ya in the bedroom is gonna be candied yams, baked macaroni and cheese, ham and potato salad with collards tender enough to melt in yo mouth. I make a red velvet cake that will raise the dead —"

"That mess oughta raise the dead, since it was that slop that probably killed them in the first place."

Bea and Trustee Noel's heads swung around. In the side door to the fellowship hall stood Sasha, one hand on her tiny hip with her cane dangling by its handle off her wrist. In her other hand, she held her customized Bible tightly.

She would have spewed more venom, but she was all out of breath. She'd figured, like Bea, that he'd be there. She looked all over the church and wasn't too happy when she found out Bea had gotten to the trustee first.

"You better believe me when I warn you it's for your own good." Sasha's eyes narrowed. The clicking sound from her tiny orthopedic shoes announced each footstep as she approached Bea and Trustee Noel.

Sasha looked him straight in his eyes as she spoke. "Even that glop that passes for food over at the Soul Food Shanty ain't built up the lining of your stomach enough to keep Bea's slop from killing you."

Before the two church mothers could lay hands on the trustee and rip him apart as Solomon threatened to do to the baby in question, Elder Batty Brick and Brother Casanova appeared. They'd arrived to make sure the hall was decorated properly, and to set up the sound system.

Trustee Noel could've kissed the men, he was that happy to see them. Alone with Bea and Sasha had never been a plan for him even if he had to go to his grave without ever having had a woman.

He fled so fast he looked like a pencil galloping out the door. Of course, when the men turned back to Bea and Sasha, they already had their excuses.

"He forgot the hangers for the coats," they said in unison.

Finally reaching the Soul Food Shanty after escaping the clutches of Bea and Sasha, he galloped up the stairs and into his room. "Oh my God!" Trustee Noel could not believe Bea and Sasha had ambushed him. They'd never said what they wanted but he was certain he knew, and just as certain he wouldn't give it to them. He'd saved himself for the right woman and neither of those two fit his limited specifications.

He thought about his Thanksgiving dinner with Sister Betty and it brought a smile to his face. She'd managed to push aside his sullen mood that only days before had pushed him to consider changing churches. His smile grew wider as he flopped down upon his small bed and disregarded the usual creaky sounds of the bedsprings.

He clapped his hands together and made a victory sign with his fingers. "*Sister Betty* and I are going to the prom together." Only he would become so overly excited at her last minute suggestion of attending together, but it didn't matter. He'd been invited somewhere by a woman he actually liked, and who had fed him once.

His face lit up again, and before he could stop, he yelled, "Thank You Heavenly Father. Thank You!"

He'd already reserved a limousine, all the way from Anderson, to take them to the prom, but he didn't have a lot of time to spend on daydreaming. Sister Betty had called him earlier and told him to be ready for a surprise or two that night. Was she ready to take it to the next level, he wondered. He wouldn't think badly of her if she did want to hold hands.

He didn't have much time to prepare, but he'd be ready and look as good as he could. He hadn't spent much of the millions, but he had gone to JCPenney and bought several suits. He just needed to choose which one to wear.

The Shanty's hot water heater still wasn't on, but he kept it moving. "A cold shower can't hurt nobody." He remained convinced until he saw the effects on his body and his limited-use manhood. Whatever Sister Betty planned, he couldn't get naked to participate.

Bea had two hours to go before she needed to arrive at the prom. She went over the final touches of her gonna-git-that-check outfit. It took her longer to stuff her girth into the outfit than she'd taken to stuff her Thanksgiving turkey. Over the years, she'd gone from a size four to a size twenty-four.

"Suck it in, Bea," she told herself as she shoved and abused her body into a sexy, one-strapped, back out, black velvet dress. She hadn't worn that dress since her fifties when she dated old Benn Dead and folded her gambling operation held in her back bedroom. That was a time when her huge breasts were about five inches off her waistline instead of their current two inches, and her back was not quite so arched.

Benn Dead was fifteen years her senior, but had the potential to make her a wealthy widow. For almost five years, she'd endured his frequent memory losses, bad breath, and need to butt trumpet the melody to "Blowin' in the Wind." Bea had given up and returned to playing bingo.

"Lord, take me back to the good ole days and further back than that old fool."

Further back were the days when she was Bea "Baby Doll" Blister, a croupier's croupier. "Have mercy, I remember a time when I would've taken Donald Trump for all his millions and held that ratty hairpiece for ransom. I'd have gotten away with it, too."

Now when she looked in a mirror, Bea's body looked the same way coming or going.

There was only one thing missing from her Bea "Baby Doll" special ensemble. Bea needed a wig and she had about ten of them spread around her bedroom. Colorful synthetic and natural hair in an array of styles were pulled down on foam wig heads and across lampshades. She finally settled upon a bright red wig with a huge green bow on its side. After all, it was the Christmas season.

Soon, she was ready to go. She'd already secured a seat on one of the church's smaller Access-A-Ride vans. She'd wanted to get there early. It wouldn't hurt if no one knew she'd arrived without a prom date.

As Bea sat by her window to watch and wait, she saw an old turkey with a broken wattle. Behind the turkey was a sleigh with a weathered Santa seated with an elf and presents. The elf figure reminded her of Sasha and the fun she'd soon have at Sasha's expense. Bea laughed until she almost shook the dress off. "Sasha's gonna have another cow to add to that herd I've already given her over the years." She really didn't know how she'd survive without her favorite foil.

Bea heard the blaring from the van's horn announcing its arrival. She felt as though she could've danced out of her home and into the street. Nobody could tell Bea she wasn't classy that night. Her huge breasts poked out so far it was hard to see that she had a hunched back.

Of course, Bea was also wearing a huge red wool hat to protect her red wig. The flapping brim blocked most of her view, which prevented her from seeing as clear as she needed, so Bea saw the van but didn't see the demon in its back seat.

When Sasha called for one of the church's vans to get to the prom, she'd learned she'd have to share the ride. "I'm in a hurry! I don't have time to stop nowhere, and I don't care who else needs a ride."

She wasn't aware that she and Bea shared the same concern. She wanted to get there early so no one would know she arrived without a prom date, too. Sasha was mad enough to chew a mud hole in a lion's butt.

She threw away her Church Mother's sanctified dress code and chose from her dusty get-a-man arsenal. None that remembered her from those times would forget how well she'd danced. Sasha "Shut 'em Down" Hellraiser was what they'd called her before she married, and later became widowed by, Hezekiah Pray Onn. Sasha called her late husband the Marlboro Man; not because he was handsome, but because he'd smoked Marlboros, and she believed cigarettes caused his death.

Determined to stay in a festive mood with new husband prospects a strong possibility, Sasha started singing. "Hellraiser parties are hot!"

From way back in her closet where she kept her way-back-in-the-day outfits she

155

rummaged until she found a two-piece, powder blue power suit. It was a Jackie Kennedy knock off from the sixties and she'd won a few dance contests with it. The jacket had a deep blue faux-fur collar with a low neckline that served no purpose other than to show the deep wrinkles on Sasha's tiny breasts.

"Have mercy, I still got it! This is gonna be like taking candy from a rich baby." She turned side-to-side and smiled with approval at her reflection in the mirror. "Yep, that po' man don't stand a chance against what I use."

Thankfully, the skirt with its six inch split on the side had a lining, because Sasha didn't always remember that panties were not optional. She accessorized it with an ecru-colored set of false teeth and matched the teeth with ecru-colored orthopedic pumps. She donned a pair of see-through plastic booties to protect the pumps from the pouring rain.

From the moment she'd entered the van Sasha raised her voice and reminded its driver of her church position, the urgency of her need, and even a lawsuit if she were late, plus anything more she could use as a warning.

Of course, the driver didn't see any economic benefits in her proposal and didn't care about her threats or comfort. But he should have.

When the van first pulled up in front of Bea's home Sasha almost stroked. Bea hadn't taken but a few steps toward the van before Sasha began to attack the poor driver. She even tried to use her cane to poke the man. "Leave that heffa where she's at and drive away!" Sasha screamed. "I ain't sharing no van with that rabid raccoon hussy! I'm head of the Mothers Board and God hears my prayers!"

"I must do a pick up at this address," the poor driver pled. "It's my job." He opened his door and was about to get out and help Bea inside when Sasha offered an ultimatum.

"Either that cow stays put on that sidewalk or I'll wrap my cane around your head."

Sasha's threat suddenly made a lot of sense to the driver and he knew he'd better make a decision, and make it quick.

Bea tried her best to act concerned, but the sight of Sasha left ranting on the sidewalk was the best early Christmas present, pre-prom gift she'd ever received. "Ya shouldn't have left that old bitter woman out on the sidewalk, sir." Bea almost choked on the words. "Ya should've just politely closed the door so *it* couldn't get all the way out of this cab."

"It was her choice, ma'am, and she threatened to beat me up if I allowed you inside."

"Oh, she said that, did she? I'm so sorry she terrorized ya. I'll speak on yo' side if you see any trouble behind this."

Bea spoke the truth that time. She was sorry — sorry that the seat was so small she couldn't turn and get a better look at Sasha's sidewalk performance.

"I'm probably gonna be sorry for this." The driver's head almost hit the steering wheel as it dropped in surrender. "I'll go back and get her."

Bea was about to issue a threat to stop him, but she was glad she didn't. It was only when the driver made a U-turn that she got a good look at the Mother Sasha Pray Onn tirade in full effect. Bea lowered the car window just enough to hear Sasha freaking out on the sidewalk. Sasha cabbage-patched, hokey-pokied and bunny hopped like a wind-up toy. Bea laughed so hard she could barely control her bladder, and was glad she'd worn a double Depend.

"I'm gonna shove this cane so far up your fat —" Sasha poked her cane at something invisible, then waved it around as if she was placing a spell on the entire town of Pelzer.

Bea had already raised the car's window but she could imagine Sasha's unkind words. "Ooh, I know that Smurf is mad!"

Turning serious, she addressed the driver. "Never mind about her, I'm trying to pray back here and that demon is a prayer blocker if ever there was one."

It didn't matter if the driver prayed or not because he had no intention of stopping. He made another U-turn and continued toward the church.

CHAPTER 17

By the time Trustee Noel finished the final touches to the new him, the limo had arrived and once inside, he couldn't stop smiling.

The rain hadn't completely stopped. Raindrops shimmered on the leafless branches of the trees. Even while riding alone in comfort and style in the Hummer limo, he couldn't stop replaying in his mind how good he'd felt when Sister Betty had suggested they spend more time together. "We need to bring Reverend Tom around," she'd said.

It seemed almost comical that at that moment his disagreement with the reverend paled next to his delight in being with Sister Betty. He intended to make the most of his first prom date.

Trustee Noel laid his head back against the limo's soft leather interior. He exhaled and then giggled again, like a schoolchild.

He'd come a long way from a janitor to where he now sat. It felt so good to relax. His head rolled from side-to-side much the way he imagined a masseuse would massage it.

As he turned and saw the outline of Pelzer's downtown area disappear among the Christmas lights and behind a few tall buildings he exhaled again. "Father, I thank You."

"Sir, we're at your destination."

Trustee Noel instructed the driver to wait while he escorted Sister Betty to the limo.

As he walked up the path to her doorway, Trustee Noel looked around the upscale and neat appearance of Sister Betty's neighborhood. He admired her again, as he'd done on Thanksgiving. God had truly blessed her with wealth and favor in her golden years, and he believed she definitely deserved it.

God had done above, and exceedingly so, for him and he was just as certain that he didn't deserve it. Why would God do that?

Sister Betty had just finished dressing in what she considered her idea of a throwback outfit. She'd chosen a white midi skirt and white blouse with billowing sleeves. She'd managed to find a pair of white stack pumps and a blond Afro wig. That wig was about as far back as she went. Salvation was all

161

she'd known for so long, she'd had to find a picture to remind her of those days.

When her doorbell rang, she gathered her Bible along with some other items for the prom. "Oh good, he's right on time." When she opened her door she found Trustee Noel waiting. He looked better than she'd ever seen him, with one exception. A JCPenney tag hung from the hem of his overcoat. She wouldn't embarrass him but she'd make certain to find a way to remove it before they arrived at the prom. "I'm so glad you showed up a little early. Let me get my coat."

Minutes later, led by stars that lit the foggy and chilly air the two seniors walked slowly down the steps from Sister Betty's house with her holding onto the trustee's arm.

"Be careful Sister Betty. You know I ain't as strong as I used to be," he warned.

Sister Betty's small frame quivered just a little as she laughed and replied, "And I ain't got nothing that will heal as quick as it used to."

Then the extremely skinny Trustee Noel laughed under his breath. He was happy for the moment that someone else accepted their limitations. He pointed to a stretch black Hummer limo and the chauffeur

162

already waiting to help them inside. "I got us a fancy car so we can ride in style."

Trustee Noel had always secretly liked Sister Betty and her unselfish friendship. He knew it came from her heart and she didn't want anything from him — except to help him help their church. His appreciation grew rapidly between her doorway and the limo.

Since entering the limousine, Sister Betty had kept quiet. It wasn't that she hadn't found everything to her liking. She just liked to listen and sometimes she could hear a person's heart and not just their words.

Finally, she smiled. "I'm happy to see that you've spent some of that money on you. The suit looks good on you." She wouldn't go so far as to tell him that he was handsome. She didn't want to diminish her prayers with a lie. He'd taken off his overcoat and laid it between them. And she secretly removed the store tag.

Trustee Noel couldn't stop grinning. "Thank you. I wasn't quite sure what to wear."

Of course, he was dressed in another JCPenney suit. He knew her remarks meant she liked it.

He was wearing a gray pinstriped suit with a lavender dress shirt. He also wore a silver tie along with a Merry Christmas tie clip. Trustee Noel topped off his newly found rich man status with a little debonair attempt at a new hairstyle. He had his little sprig of hair polished with lacquer spray and he smelled as though he'd bathed in Old Spice and pig's feet. Living over the Soul Food Shanty gave him an odor nothing could mask.

"Sister Betty," he said suddenly as he turned his head away from her. "Do you mind if I ask you a question?"

The change caught her off guard. She didn't understand how he'd gone from happy to apparently glum in a few seconds. Was it something she'd said or did? "Why certainly, what's on your mind?"

"I'm not ungrateful or anything," Trustee Noel continued. His voice halted as he reached up and nervously began twirling his lacquered sprig, setting off tiny lacquer missiles around the backseat. "I brought my old janitor uniform with me to wear as a throwback to my former days. Working was all I ever did so there wasn't much to choose from. Should I have worn it instead of what I'm wearing? I wasn't sure what you'd wear and I didn't want us to arrive looking foolish."

"And you made a decision based on what

you thought I'd wear?" Sister Betty tried not to laugh, but he was acting so sweet. She could tell he was nervous and that became endearing so she didn't ask him to show his uniform. At that very moment, she began to feel like a young girl on a date. It had been so long since she'd had male company, other than a relative or her pastor. It took a moment for her to relax in the company of a man, even an unattractive one, and accept his compliment.

Over Christmas carols, coming from the limousine's radio, the two seniors sat back, relaxed and laughed. All the years they'd attended the same church yet they really didn't know one another that well. As the rain continued to fall and mixed with the silence of the evening and a lit sky allowed just a hint of light inside the limousine, they chatted away. The conversation was about nothing in particular, but not once did either mention Reverend Tom or the twenty-five million dollars.

After they'd ridden a ways, Trustee Noel stopped twisting his sprig hair and assumed a rather take charge look. He straightened his shoulders and turned down the volume. He slid over a little closer to Sister Betty, crossed his legs, rested his hands upon his knees and whispered, "Sister Betty, you look very pretty tonight."

He couldn't seem to take his eyes away from the blond Afro wig she wore. "I don't think I've ever seen you throw back like this."

Neither could hold it in. They laughed at his feeble attempt at flattery and seduction. "Well, as long as I don't throw back nothing else tonight, whether it's a drink or dance, I'm good," Sister Betty finally replied.

Then, just that quick, the laughter died and Trustee Noel's mood turned suddenly somber. "I'm not sure what's expected from me tonight. I don't want to come off as snobby but I don't want folks trying to get next to me for the wrong reasons." He reached over and pulled out a silver box with a bow on it. "I almost forgot your corsage."

Trustee Noel clumsily pulled a wrist corsage with a medium sized carnation in its center. He slipped it on her small wrist and gave the cheesiest grin when he saw how much she liked it.

"This is just lovely," Sister Betty said as she examined the flower. "And it's real, too."

As much as she wanted to continue praising him for his thoughtfulness, she couldn't take her eyes off the larger box that remained on the seat. "What's in the other box? I hope you don't mind me asking."

"That's the costume I mentioned. It's my old janitor uniform." Trustee Noel winked. "I'm gonna get down, get funky, and get loose. I'll change after we get there."

"Do you really consider that a throwback to what you were?" Sister Betty struggled to find words to explain how ridiculous the notion was that he'd been nothing but a janitor. She couldn't.

She really didn't have to because something more ridiculous caught their attention.

Sister Betty and Trustee Noel came upon Sasha just as they'd driven past Bea's house. They heard Sasha's big mouth through the limo's closed and supposedly soundproof window. She was fussing, cussing, and spinning like an out of control demon on Bea's sidewalk.

It took Sister Betty a moment to believe her eyes and ears. When she finally did, she hollered and warned the driver, "Don't stop!" But the trustee being forever the resident gentleman and a fool made the driver pull over.

Once they'd gotten her calmed down, Sasha gave her version of what led to her outside and unpaid performance. "Bea's fault," she ranted. "That hippo threatened the van's driver and made him toss me out onto the street. She only did it 'cause she's a desperate hussy. Bea just wanted a man and she didn't care if it was a piss-po' van driver. That She-Rilla just wanted to ride alone with the man."

"Somehow I believe you just might be leaving out a few details," Sister Betty said once they'd gotten Sasha's walking cane secured in the back seat of the limousine. She'd spun like a helicopter rotor before then and threatened to decapitate something or someone.

"I'm sure there's a more reasonable explanation." Reasonable in Sister Betty's mind meant truthful. She didn't doubt for a moment that Sasha lied, but they needed to get to the prom.

In the meantime, Trustee Noel sat back and eyed Sasha's cane. He wanted to grab it and whip his own behind with it. After her performance earlier that day, when would he ever learn?

CHAPTER 18

Before the limousine even pulled up in front of the church, Trustee Noel wanted to pay a hit man to put either him or Sasha out of their misery. He'd already borrowed several painkillers from the limo driver and downed them with glasses of Pepsi cola.

"I don't believe soft drinks and aspirin go together," Sister Betty warned. "They can make you feel a little extra something you ain't."

Putting up with Sasha's constant griping or getting a slight buzz caused him to ignore Sister Betty's advice. By the time they arrived for the Seniors Prom, the three of them were out of sorts. Trustee Noel laughed like a hyena, Sasha made crabs seem nicer, and Sister Betty pocketed two painkillers just in case.

No one who'd ever been inside the Crossing Over Sanctuary Fellowship Hall before would've recognized it on Seniors Prom night. It screamed of chic cheap from the doorway to the back exit.

Brother Casanova had gathered a few of the other church brothers and decked the hall with boughs of whatever he borrowed from the drama department. Red, blue, yellow, and white lights hung all along the walls, windows, and doors. Some of the lights borrowed from a Christmas play flashed on and off. Between the flashing lights and the huge spinning silver Disco ball hung from the ceiling in the middle of the room, hypnotism would surely play a big role this night. And surprisingly enough Brother Casanova had found a few wreaths of mistletoe. He'd hung them way off in a corner to keep Bea happy.

The prom started at about eight-thirty and most of the guests had arrived by then. Elder Batty Brick and his questionable math skills had outsold capacity. Always the optimist, he figured with a few not too fatal heart attacks and others being lost going to the bathroom or returning to the Senior Center by ten o'clock, there'd be plenty of room.

He couldn't have been more wrong. For weeks, those old folk did their homework. They'd pulled out old photograph albums

170

and yearbooks. Whoever knew how to went online and researched their names to see whether there was a bit of scandal attached. Notoriety would elevate their status and make it seem as though they'd lived the high life or did something worth mentioning on prom night.

One thing was for certain, when they came through the door, many had one thing in mind. The seniors wanted a little piece of Heaven while they partied in Egypt.

Of course, some of Bea and Sasha's moneymaking schemes backfired. The inclement weather made their efforts to cash in on parking scooters and wheelchairs a bust. Those seniors had already pooled their pennies and rented buses. Belton, South Carolina didn't have more than about nine hundred eligible seniors over the age of fifty-five and they were represented twenty-five percent. Anyone in Belton needing a babysitter that night was out of luck.

Piedmont, Williamston, Pickens, and Oconee, South Carolina were represented well, too. Seniors in various stages of mental and physical health or decay had arrived in long and short yellow buses. Of course, that didn't bode well for the evening.

The elevators soon went out of service due to the overload, yet nothing kept the attendees from their mission. It took a little longer, but the elderly poured or limped into the fellowship hall. They came dressed to impress, too. The old folks wore everything from Afro puffs to gangster leans and Mack Daddy fur-collared long coats.

Some not too certain how old they were wore flapper costumes as though they could knock knees together without fracturing something.

Of course, there were a few seniors so bold as to arrive at the prom in orthopedic platform shoes. No sooner had they handed in their tickets and tried to walk on the slippery floor, than they fell. They went immediately to the local hospital emergency room with sprained ankles and swollen feet. That narrowed the crowd down a bit and left plenty of room for dancing.

Not to be outdone, Crossing Over Sanctuary's Mothers and Trustees Board Members stole the show. Many wore their minis and a few wore fedoras and KangaROOS. Whatever hustle they hustled in the past was on display. It soon began to look more like a Playa's Ball than a Seniors Prom.

The Deacon Board showed up and showed out. Some of the old playas thought a throwback party meant they could throw back like they were still single. Well, they

172

weren't. A few well-placed knee kicks to their groins from their wives on the Deaconess Board jolted them back to reality.

Several of the trustees needed their private packages publicly iced. They also went to the emergency room, leaving more room on the dance floor.

In the meantime, Sister Betty and Trustee Noel waded through a crowd of gawkers and gossipers. She tried her best to make the trustee walk steady but those painkillers only made his gallop worse. She looked like she was leading a horse to a barn — an unwilling horse, because the trustee kept pulling back and clawing at Sasha who walked a little too close to his hind quarters.

Sasha took it as a hint that the trustee wanted to fight, but she liked her victims sober. She scurried off to find Bea so she could harass her, but not before the braggarts, liars, and busybodies had their say.

And the biggest braggart, liar, and busybody set it off.

Elder Batty Brick had stood the test of time and a few paternity tests, too. He'd told Bea and Sasha that back in the day he'd owned the dance floor. He hadn't told a total lie. He did pay for the wooden floor when he owned the Tin Pan Alley Cat Club. That was before the feds shut it down for

173

trafficking in whatever was illegal at that time.

To get things started Elder Batty Brick gave the welcome prayer and then asked, "Will one of you fine ladies like to start off the prom with me?"

"I most certainly would." The response came from one of the tables in the back where the mistletoe hung. It was Alice "Grandma Puddin' " Tart. "Let me show you how it's done."

Alice "Grandma Puddin' " inched her way toward Elder Batty Brick. She wore purple house slippers, and a purple poodle felt skirt with a wide crinoline to make the skirt spread out. Every few feet she stopped and waved to the onlookers who looked at her as if she'd lost her remaining bit of mind.

It seemed that old Alice had opened her welcome pack a little early. She'd seen Bea's handwritten T-shirt that read NO VIAGRA — SEE ALICE INSTEAD.

Alice "Grandma Puddin'," so over-whelmed that someone would remember how she once lay it down thanked Bea and gave her a hug. "Bea, baby, back in the day men folk didn't know 'bout that Viagra but they knew to see Alice." She couldn't thank Bea enough for not forgetting her throwback skill. And to show just how much she loved the Lord for saving her, Alice had immediately put on the shirt; but she hadn't worn a bra.

Brother Casanova thought the whole thing comical so he rushed and threw on an old BBD CD. Within a few seconds, the track to "That Girl is Poison" rang out over the fellowship hall.

Well, old Alice, no more than a hundred pounds if she were wet, put a hurting on Elder Batty Brick. It was as if that T-shirt had magical or healing powers. Near ninety years old, she recalled every trick in her book. Old mother Alice "Grandma Puddin' " smacked it up, flipped it, flopped it, and when she finished, she rubbed him on down.

"Oh no, do me baby!" Elder Batty Brick hollered as he waved his arms in the air and acted like he just didn't care.

Well old Alice "Grandma Puddin' " worked it some more. In no time she Bell, Biv'd and Devoe'd him without getting out of breath, then dragged him away to check out the mistletoe.

It took Elder Batty Brick several minutes to recover from Alice's workout. While still lathered with sweat, he continued to emcee the rest of the program.

Not many paid attention to his lame jokes

and throwback history after Alice turned him out.

When the male stripper Bea hired, an eighty-year-old Vietnamese fella named Hung Lo, hit the stage, the seniors moved in closer. He lived in her building and claimed that in the sixties he'd stripped back in the Mekong Delta. He never told her that he'd done it at the end of a bayonet.

Anyway, old Hung Lo lowered the wrong set of balls under the belt he wore around his skinny waist. Pandemonium broke out. The old mothers lost it, the old trustees searched for it, and Bea collected money from those who'd tried to feel to see if Hung Lo's were real or Memorex.

After a while, the seniors started buzzing and recreating stories about Sister Betty dragging Trustee Noel through the door and disappearing out of sight.

"I thought she was rich," snorted one of the seniors. "I guess while the rest of us suffer she done latched onto the richest sucker at the church." The observation came from an elderly woman who apparently thought that back in the day she was Diana Ross. She came dressed in a flimsy sequined mini dress and bouffant black wig with wing tips. Dark, scary mascara circled her eyes. It might've worked except Sister Mae Ling was Chinese. She didn't go through U.S. customs until the mid-nineties. By then Diana Ross was no longer the boss.

Of course, the conversation segued into "He looked like he'd been drinking. He was probably drunk. I always figured somebody had to get drunk to deal with Sister Betty." That conclusion came from the lips of many.

When Sister Betty finally got him to stop galloping, it took prayer and a lot of it to bring Trustee Noel to his senses. "Please don't ever do that again," Sister Betty warned. The evening barely got started and they were about to have their first spat. But they didn't. Sister Betty took Trustee Noel to an empty seat where the crowded dance floor hid them from view.

"I'm sorry," Trustee Noel whispered. "Sasha has always scared me, but tonight she made me hopping mad."

"Hopping mad?" Sister Betty hadn't heard that phrase in years and coming from Trustee Noel all she could do was laugh. "Don't worry about it. We got bigger fish to fry."

"Did your friend show up yet?" Trustee Noel's eyes followed Sister Betty's as she scanned the crowd. Although he had no idea who she looked for, each time her eyes stopped, his did, too.

A few moments later the concerned expression on Sister Betty's face relaxed. "Come on," Sister Betty told the trustee as she stood. "I see my special guest."

CHAPTER 19

Brother Casanova wanted the seniors out on the dance floor. He knew just how to do it. He reached into his satchel and pulled out a handful of CDs, flipping through them until he found the one throwback jam that would raise folks from a dirt sleep. "This one's for all the throwbacks who threw back without throwing their backs out. Come on church folk, 'Le Freak' with Chic."

At first, it sounded like a cattle stampede. Shoes and canes of every sort made clicking sounds as the seniors rushed to the floor, although by the time some made it half the song had played.

Most of the seniors danced until they dropped, and the rest just stepped over them and continued dancing a combination of the butterfly, the can-can, and the laffy taffy. There were several with hip replacements who still managed to form an electric slide line and those who could dip did so.

All their moves were homage to Le Freak. But then the ever playful Brother Casanova decided they hadn't enough. "Aww, don't stop now. Y'all ain't threw back enough. Just push the rest of those Has-Beens to the side, and see how ya handle this next one."

Along with one CD after another, Brother Casanova danced a little jig inside his clapboard DJ booth and worked those oldsters. From Aretha's "Rock Steady" and Chubby Checker's "The Twist" to Labelle's "Lady Marmalade," Brother Casanova gave them flashbacks enough for a lifetime. When he saw they were slayed by the spirit of music, he ended that segment with his signature theme song, Ruby Andrews' "Casanova (Your Playing Days Are Over)."

In the meantime, Sister Betty and Trustee Noel swam through the crowd of dancers. They sometimes pushed aside canes, walkers, and folks that never should've been on the dance floor.

Sister Betty suddenly stopped. She nodded to Trustee Noel and led him toward the corner where a woman sat alone.

"May we join you, Congresswoman Bigelow?" Sister Betty waited for the old woman to give a signal that she at least knew someone spoke to her.

"Sister Betty, you know I don't drop drawers for Washington politicians anymore. I don't know how many times I hafta tell you to just call me Cheyenne, please."

"Of course," Sister Betty replied. She'd forgotten just how uninhibited the old woman was. "May we sit down?"

"Wasn't that what y'all were about to do before those geriatric old fools danced and went crazy?" Former Congresswoman Cheyenne nodded toward the empty seats next to her and added, "You know you can hear a lot when you watch closely."

Trustee Noel and Sister Betty sat down with the congresswoman seated in their middle. Sister Betty introduced the trustee to the former congresswoman.

Trustee Noel managed to nod coyly at the woman introduced as Cheyenne. He didn't want to stare, but found he couldn't turn away. He gathered by her demeanor she was a very unusual woman.

Cheyenne Bigelow was just slightly older than Sister Betty. She had an extremely long, bluish-tinged braid that rested over her shoulder. She wore a short pink dress, revealing blue spidery veins on her thighs that matched her ice-blue eyes. She caught the trustee staring at her and raised her flask to toast something invisible followed by a deep swig.

Sister Betty put her hand to her mouth and coughed. When the trustee looked her way, she twisted her mouth to show her displeasure. She wanted him to stop staring at Cheyenne.

Once she'd gotten the trustee back on track, Sister Betty spoke. "It's been quite some time since we saw each other at the Seniors Prom a few months ago." She didn't want to raise her voice over the loud music so she moved her chair closer and motioned for the trustee to do the same. "You look amazing and well."

Then she changed the subject. "I'm sorry about asking you to meet me here. I'd forgotten how loud the music would be. This was supposed to be a Seniors Prom gathering to remember the old times."

"You weren't too far off the mark; especially that part about remembering the old." Cheyenne's eye's twinkled as she leaned in and conspired. "These are old church folks, after all." She spun her cane around and pointed toward the spot where Elder Batty Brick had returned to continue with the program. "I see my favorite embezzler is still on the Lord's side. I hope the Lord is still counting the money after that old swindler collects it."

Sister Betty wanted to speak but she

didn't. She was too happy that Cheyenne came out that night and was in such a good mood.

When they'd last seen one another in Belton, Cheyenne had dropped some interesting if not downright ridiculous tidbits on Sister Betty. The way Cheyenne had spoken at the Belton Seniors Prom as she sneaked a sip or two from a silver liquor flask told Sister Betty that the old woman didn't care for some of her own church members. She called them "hypocritical geriatric fluff." And although he wasn't old, after a few more long swigs that time from her flask, Cheyenne hadn't had too many good things to say about Reverend Tom, either.

Sister Betty had dismissed Cheyenne's observations due to the flask, especially when she'd ranted about the reverend's high moral standards. "Reverend Leotis Tom needs to come down off his high horse before that same high horse tosses his arse. Even his grandmamma didn't act all high-falutin."

Sister Betty, mired in her recall moment, forgot she sat in the present and didn't realize her jaw had dropped.

"Don't look so shocked at me swigging from this flask." Cheyenne turned to Trustee Noel and winked. "This ain't nothing but

183

some tea with lemon and honey." She then swung back around to Sister Betty and added, "You've forgotten that acting crazy was how I kept getting reelected. And Lord knows, crazy would be a qualification for certain nowadays."

Sister Betty said what she was certain was on the trustee's mind as well. "Why do you need to act senile? Has someone said or done something to you?"

Cheyenne cackled and tapped her side. "Honey, please. This rheumatoid arthritis may have my joints, but I'd still shoot any summa-gun before I'd let him scare me. I've been in politics long enough to know you gotta hold your cards close to the chest."

Sister Betty softened her voice and asked, "Even with your own church and such, you need to do that?"

"Actually, I'm especially leery when it comes down to *your* church and its leader, more so than mine."

Cheyenne picked up her flask. She pretended to drink and made a motion showing she was checking out her surroundings. She again turned to Trustee Noel. She pushed her seat closer and leaned in to whisper in his ear.

When Cheyenne pulled away from the trustee, he immediately started pulling on

184

his sprig. Sister Betty realized whatever she'd said, she'd made him more nervous than Sasha ever could, but she didn't want to come across as jealous so she said nothing.

"And Trustee Noel" — Cheyenne turned back and looked him square in his eye — "you make sure that when you go and get my plate none of the green food touches anything that's yellow, like an ear of corn. Separate it if they're serving succotash."

"Yes, ma'am. I'll be certain your food is segregated."

"And you also make sure that the icing on my red velvet cake isn't running over more than an inch from the top. You got that?"

"Yes, ma'am, not more than an inch," Trustee Noel nodded. "Can I do anything more for you?"

"No, I don't need anything else. You just remember what I told you. I still have friends and connections with the IRS. They may wanna talk to you about all that money you just got.

"That oughta give him something to do and think about for a while." Turning toward Sister Betty after the trustee was completely out of sight, Cheyenne added, "I believe you need a toilet break." She reached for her cane. "I know I do, and we

185

could use the privacy. C'mon. Ain't nobody gonna look twice at two old women trying not to wet their drawers."

While they walked toward the hallway bathroom, Cheyenne stopped and used her cane to point toward the kitchen. "I almost forgot to tell you. When you first sat down Bea and Sasha were going at it. Those two old clucking hens should've been plucked long ago."

Trustee Noel's nerves were so shot he'd forgotten he hadn't put on his janitor throwback outfit. He would have to carry plates of food back from the buffet line and hope none spilled on his new JCPenney suit. He couldn't believe how things had changed since he'd first picked up Sister Betty for the prom.

He hadn't felt this let down since he'd overheard his grandma telling his grade school teacher to sit him in the back of the room. "If you sit Freddie away from the pretty students they may not laugh and tease him so much because he ain't cute." It would not have hurt so much if his grandmother wasn't blind and had never laid an eye on him.

And now he was a millionaire still living in a roach motel. Added to his misery, he had to play fetch for some crazy expolitician's quirky feeding fetish. He began seriously to rethink the idea of moving his membership and his body out of Pelzer completely. Maybe he'd save a lot of heartache if he did, especially if he could convince Sister Betty to leave, too.

The trustee had just passed the kitchen on his way toward the buffet line when all hell broke loose. As soon as he heard their voices, he knew BS had started.

"You knew those were my teeth in that glass when you emptied it into the sink," Sasha screamed above the music as she pointed her cane to accuse Bea of the travesty.

"Why the ham and cheese did ya put them in a doggone glass in the first place? They looked like a nasty piece of gingerroot to me." Bea moved from side to side as she dodged the business end of Sasha's cane. Her wide hips knocked pots and pans off the counter.

"It ain't none of your business why!" Sasha poked at Bea the same as she would the middle of a piece of fried baloney. She jabbed at Bea and missed again. "You old blind battle ax."

Bea dodged again and screamed, "I forgot ya don't know nothing about teeth with ya baldheaded mouth."

187

"I may be old but you are an educated ignoramus and you can't read," Sasha screamed. "You so ignorant you spread KY Jelly on a biscuit. You couldn't see or taste the difference, either!"

The two old women spilled out from the kitchen onto the dance floor.

Brother Casanova threw on "Kung Fu Fighting" to give the scuffle some flava.

"Oh hell!" The words escaped Sister Betty's mouth before she could pull them or Cheyenne back to safety.

Watching Bea and Sasha go at it was like watching old reruns. The ending never changed and collateral damages always occurred.

One minute after Bea and Sasha squared off, Elder Batty Brick fled the floor and Brother Casanova finally stopped the music.

Trying to play it off as a joke, Elder Batty Brick laughed slightly and said over the microphone, "Well, never let it be said that the Mothers Board at Crossing Over Sanctuary don't know how to entertain. I believe even Lucifer has gathered his demons to watch and learn a thing or two."

Since Brother Casanova hadn't adjusted his hearing aide since he entered the door, he didn't know what Elder Batty Brick said or how dumb it sounded. So he threw on the theme song to a Rocky movie and turned up the volume.

Suddenly, one side of the room cleared and everybody pulled out their cell phones with their fingers on speed dial to call the cops, or the local television news desk if necessary. Several seniors had their hands on unlicensed pistols. Meanwhile Cheyenne went on to the bathroom because she really needed to go.

Sister Betty waved her Bible around aiming it like a machine gun. With her free hand, she pulled her spray canister of blessed oil from her bag.

But BS continued.

"Ya got a lot of nerve lying on me like that. Ya rabid old Smurf." Bea looked around. She needed to see if Sasha's KY Jelly accusation had an effect.

Everyone had a deadpan look and tried acting as if they weren't interested even though they stared real hard at her.

Bea spun around to face Sasha again. She'd turned so fast she was already facing Sasha by the time her huge wiggling breasts caught up.

"I smell somethin'." Bea stopped and sniffed the air before addressing Sasha again. "Ya stink. Everyone knows yo' ugly dress made outta Doctor Scholl's Odor Eaters."

And that's when all except Sister Betty put away his or her cell phones. Church folks and a few alley cats who paid at the door pulled out paper cups, shot glasses, and flasks from their hips. The alcohol percentages were high at that moment. Cups and flasks filled with everything from Pepsi to Smirnoff, and anywhere from 10 percent to one hundred and eighty proof magically appeared. Everyone, including Cheyenne Bigelow, who'd returned from the bathroom, took a deep swig or two and found a seat to watch the showdown that was already in progress.

Bea and Sasha started moving toward each other, but they moved so slow by the time they came face-to-face, they'd forgotten why they fought.

Just as one of the church mothers was about to rumble, the door to the fellowship hall opened.

Sister Betty stood closest to the door and it took a moment to realize who stood there. "Oh my Lord!" She didn't mean to yell so loud, but she had. Naturally, all eyes left the BS fight and turned to see what had caused the fear in her words.

"Reverend Tom?" Sister Betty didn't have

to finish the sentence. He entered with his coat unbuttoned and his face unshaved, and looked as though he'd already been in a fight and lost badly.

Cheyenne leaned on her cane and whispered to Sister Betty, "This is how a fool looks when he thinks too highly of himself."

CHAPTER 20

"Pastor!" Further words were unnecessary as Sister Betty's feet moved ahead of her mind. She wasted no time in rushing toward the door. It was hard to tell by her stride and the way she knocked over a few chairs if she even realized she'd dropped her Bible onto a table and the blessed oil canister on the floor.

While the others stood dazed and undecided, Trustee Noel quickly put aside his displeasure with his pastor and made a move. His skinny body wound through the crowd like a snake. In just a few seconds, he joined Sister Betty, who'd already reached the reverend's side.

"We weren't expecting you," Sister Betty said as she led the pastor to an empty seat. She wanted to say more, but by that time, Cheyenne had joined them.

"It makes no sense at all," Sister Betty whispered. "He said he wouldn't come. He was on a shut-in."

Trustee Noel paid no attention to what Sister Betty questioned. His pastor looked terrible. Grabbing a water glass off the table, the trustee filled it and offered it to the reverend.

Reverend Tom accepted the water and after taking a few sips, he looked around the room and waved his hand over the crowd, but he still did not speak.

Trustee Noel stepped back a few feet to see what would happen next. He wasn't too certain about his pastor's reaction once the man realized who'd given him the drink of water.

It wasn't that Trustee Noel thought his pastor would flip over a cup of something cold to drink, as he had over a twenty-five million dollar tithe offering, but Trustee Noel had seen enough drama for the night. He turned and galloped to the other side of the fellowship hall. All that did was place him with the ones he least wanted to be near, Bea and Sasha.

The only way to stop the gawking was to start the Bachelor Auction. The seniors began to bid on hope, faith, and some of the most uncharitable bachelors around. Sasha had promised some of the single women she'd stack the deck in their favor and she did. It wasn't ten minutes after the bidding closed and the winners were announced that Sasha placed high on the top of their hit list.

One of the singles, Miss Vickie, who was also a Christian comedienne, had flown all the way from Dallas for a shot at matrimony. Perhaps she wasn't specific enough about the man she wanted. Miss Vickie was all of five feet nine. Her bachelor was shy of five feet by about five inches. Miss Vickie accepted the additional sky miles added to her winnings, hoisted the short fella onto her shoulder and carried him out of there.

Meanwhile Sister Betty and Cheyenne took the reverend into the hallway. Walking toward the elevator to his office. Sister Betty spoke. "Glad to see you did come," she said for the second time. She was surprised he finally answered.

"I only came because Miss Cheyenne called and said you needed me."

"I needed you?" Sister Betty turned from her pastor and looked at Cheyenne, who walked away and pressed the elevator button without saying a word.

"You don't need me?" Reverend Tom's face was a mask of silent questions. He looked worse than he did ten minutes ago.

The elevator door opened and Sister

Betty, Reverend Tom, and Cheyenne entered.

When they were in the study they sat for a moment and allowed their minds to clear. The music was still a little loud and they could hear murmurings from the seniors below. It wasn't enough to interfere with a conversation, but was just enough to let them know there was a party going on.

Cheyenne finally admitted that she'd called Reverend Tom even before Sister Betty and Trustee Noel had approached her table. The reverend hadn't seemed agreeable when she first asked him to counsel her about a problem she supposedly had. However, as soon as she threw Sister Betty's name into the mix, he agreed to show up. She apologized for using trickery to get him to come and prefaced it by telling him it was for his good as well as his church.

From the way the reverend appeared, disheveled and out of sorts, they could only guess that his fast and prayer hadn't gone quite the way he'd wanted.

"You don't have that glow that comes from being alone with the Lord," Sister Betty observed. "I don't hear the shout of victory coming off your lips or see the glint of favor in your eyes."

"That's because it's not there." The rever-

195

end hung his head. "I'm only trying to do what's right."

"Do what's right for whom?" Cheyenne wasn't a member of Crossing Over Sanctuary but her question cut and when she asked she looked the reverend square in his eyes. She spoke as if her tithes paid the mortgage.

"Cheyenne," Sister Betty blurted. "This is a man of God."

Cheyenne never took her eyes off Reverend Tom. Her defiant look dared him to speak. "This man may be a man of God," she snapped, "but this man is a fraud."

CHAPTER 21

Time passed since Cheyenne's accusation, yet no one made a sound inside Reverend Tom's study. Only the outside grunts of old buses warming up to await passengers filtered through the closed windows.

Sister Betty had wanted to confront Cheyenne earlier to learn what she meant when she made that same claim in Belton, but with everything going awry at the prom, she hadn't done so. Now, in the midst of her pastor's worst moments, her dear friend had delivered an accusation so close to an impeachment that Sister Betty thought she'd faint.

If Reverend Tom wanted to remain a pastor in good standing and of high spiritual fiber he should've just kept his mouth shut like he'd done since he arrived. But he didn't. Cheyenne had pushed his hot button and he let go.

"Miss Bigelow," Reverend Tom said

slowly, "I'm not accustomed to having disagreements with my senior members —"

"Liar," Cheyenne replied. "You don't know nothing about your seniors to disagree or agree with them."

He clenched his teeth and his fists. His eyes swept around his study for something to toss before she became that something to toss. "Woman, you know nothing about me!"

"I know more than you think I know about you!" Cheyenne rose using her cane for support. She put one hand on her hip and whipped her long braid around as though it were a karate move. "I know your grandmother Lillie Sinclair was a whore! I know Lillie Sinclair left your family well-off. And I know Lillie Sinclair's money sent you to that fancy divinity college."

A swooshing sound went through the study and sucked out all the air along with it.

"You're a liar!" The reverend's pecan-colored complexion darkened and his eyes turned into ebony orbs. Since the woman didn't respect his anointing he decided he'd lay it down for a moment. Reverend Tom used words that came close to cussing and laid her out. It seemed that over the past few weeks he'd become good at it.

While Reverend Tom and Cheyenne Big-elow went at it, Sister Betty retreated to a chair in the corner. Her eyes darted from side to side as she waited for someone to rush in and holler, "Cut, it's a wrap." It all seemed like a movie and a very bad one at that.

But if it was a bad movie there were plenty of folks to take the credit. Cheyenne made sure that they did.

"Well, I see you inherited Lillie's filthy mouth and her combative spirit. That's good. Perhaps, you'll use both when you take your stubborn self-righteousness and deposit them along with that twenty-five million dollars that you ignorantly refused."

"The Devil is a liar!" The reverend tossed a few books against the wall nearly slapping Sister Betty upside her head with them.

"Oh, that's good, too. Lillie had that same fire. I remember when she'd cut a John if he was a penny short."

Reverend Tom began to lose moral ground with every accusation. First, it was Bea and her claim that most of the tithes had some sort of tainted beginning. Now this woman claimed his grandmother was a whore. He knew his grandmother Lillie to be a very successful businesswoman who'd died of a stroke when he was a young boy. He refused to believe she'd left him money from prostitution or that it had sent him to the pulpit. There was no way that all these years he'd preached and pastored God's untarnished word was embedded in tainted money.

But what if Miss Cheyenne was wrong, he thought. Sister Betty and she are friends. Surely, my spiritual mother would've said something, especially since she sided with the trustee about his money.

Somehow, Sister Betty's silence gave him hope. Cheyenne Bigelow, on the other hand, was an old politician relic.

The reverend's angry face morphed into one that smiled. He apologized. "I'm sorry for my bad choice in words. I'm asking you and God to please forgive me."

"It didn't bother me none," Cheyenne replied. "I know some preachers who come through the door cussing and don't stop until they say amen."

"That may be with some preachers Cheyenne, but that's not how my pastor runs God's church." Sister Betty had finally found her voice. She'd heard enough to understand what Cheyenne had tried to tell her back in Belton. But what she didn't have was the proof. Cheyenne would need to prove those accusations to her.

Sister Betty looked at Cheyenne and

Reverend Tom. Both seemed resolute. Did they both know just a little of the truth, but not all? She felt a headache coming on and then her left knee started twitching. It hadn't twitched in a few days and it happening now was not a good sign.

As if Cheyenne read their minds, she said, "I guess y'all probably wondering who else would know about Lillie's money-making skills and her benevolent spirit."

"That would help." Reverend Tom had already decided he'd humor the woman because something about what she'd revealed bothered him. Not all of it had to do with his grandmother. Some had to do with him.

"Well, you'd better buckle up son, because if anyone knows about your grandmother's wanton ways, I certainly do."

Cheyenne stopped speaking and motioned to the reverend that she'd like one of the Vitamin Waters he had off to the side of his desk. "Could you make mine a pomegranate and blueberry? I'm trying to keep what little health I got at my age."

The reverend did as she asked and after he took off the cap and handed it to her she produced her flask and poured the water in it.

Cheyenne threw her head back and in an

instant, she'd wrapped her long braid about her head and swigged from the flask. "From what I've read and heard, you've been acting like you are about to lose your mind and the Promised Land, too."

She leaned forward on her cane and narrowed her eyes in his and Sister Betty's direction. The way she'd done it was more conspiring than she'd meant, but she would have her say.

"You sir, Reverend Leotis Tom, need to come down off your high horse before that same high horse tosses your butt and tramples you. Even your grandmamma, a bigger whore than me, didn't act all high-falutin. The difference was she made her money on her back for those fancy pants in Charleston. I made mine on my back serving up those sleazy geezers on Capitol Hill. Lillie made more money than me, too."

If there'd been a fireplace in the pastor's study, the flames couldn't singe Sister Betty more than Cheyenne's hot words of accusation about the reverend's grandmother. "You mean Reverend Tom's grandmother truly was a . . ." Sister Betty couldn't say the word.

Cheyenne chuckled and took another swig from the flask. Replacing the cap, she turned toward the reverend.

"Poor Reverend Tom. Here you are unable to suspend your disbelief. You probably didn't know that about your grandmother. If memory serves me I believe Lillie died while you was still crapping in diapers and both your parents followed each other to the grave soon after."

Cheyenne rested the cane against the chair's armrest and sat back. "I'm getting ready to tell you a story. And the best way for me to do that is to tell it to you like you wasn't Lillie's grandbaby. It makes it a little easier to tell it that way, especially since I don't have too much animosity for you."

"Yes ma'am." The reverend felt as whipped as when he'd fought that angel in his living room. He couldn't raise a fist if his life depended upon it. What had he done to God to deserve this?

"Reverend Tom," Cheyenne said softly, "why don't you turn on your security monitor and fix it so it shows the fellowship hall and those seniors. That way if anything crazier than what's already happened pops up, you'll know about it. And that way you can pay attention to what I'm about to say, too.

"Sister Betty, why don't you move a little closer so I don't have to raise my voice or repeat something. If the clock on that wall is correct the fellowship hall should be shutting down about now." Cheyenne waited until the reverend turned on the monitor and set the split screen to show inside the hall and outside in the parking lot.

"Well," Cheyenne said as she took another swig from the flask, "I don't hear any police sirens so I guess nobody pulled a weapon or anybody but Bea and Sasha fought tonight."

Nervous laughter filled the space words left empty, and Sister Betty moved her chair closer and sat down next to Reverend Tom.

"Lillie Sinclair was the absentee mama of Leotis' mama, Helena. I believe there wasn't too much of a maternal relationship between Lillie and Helena." Cheyenne spoke directly to Reverend Tom as though she were continuing from where she left off. "Helena never raised Leotis but Helena's sister-in-law Mabel Tom did after Helena passed away."

Cheyenne stopped and laughed softly. "Who am I kidding? The truth was that Lillie Sinclair was a whoring hustler who made Jezebel, Delilah, and me all look like angels. Lillie Sinclair put whoring on the map back in Charleston and made a ton of money for a lot of folks when she'd done it."

If Cheyenne noticed that the reverend flinched every time she mentioned the words *whore* or *whore's money,* she didn't show it. She just kept right on telling the story as though narrating about somebody they didn't all know.

For the next ten minutes while Sister Betty and Reverend Tom sat shocked, dismayed, and yet amazed, Cheyenne gave a history lesson on the Reverend Tom's family, especially his maternal grandmother Lillie.

"My father's people raised me after my parents died." Reverend Tom rose and paced. "No one has ever once mentioned anything negative about her family. They were mostly college-educated and very religious."

"It don't surprise me none," Cheyenne replied. "I'm sure those uppity Toms tried to rewrite your history. They'd sooner have you believe that you were a test-tube baby than tell you about your Grandma Lillie's scandalous ways. But those Toms were the biggest hypocrites of all."

"Why would you say that?" Sister Betty had learned so much in such a short time she wasn't sure why she wanted to know more.

"Why would I say that?" Cheyenne's eyes narrowed and she pointed at Sister Betty and then to the reverend. "Let me tell y'all

205

something. When I was a whore I was a proud one. I didn't try to hide who or what I was. Now those Toms, they didn't just try to hide stuff, they buried it all the way down to China."

"I don't understand where you're going with this. What does it have to do with me?" Reverend Tom asked.

"I know this is your office, but please don't interrupt. I'm honestly having too much fun, if not mixed with a little anger in revealing this."

Cheyenne reached over and snatched a handful of Christmas Kisses from a candy dish before she continued. She spoke as she unraveled the silver foil in much the same way she unraveled the truth about Reverend Tom.

"I don't know how to make this any plainer, but let me sum this up for you. You, reverend, are who you are and where you are because Lillie Sinclair laid on her back, then willed her wealth to her only grandson. Lillie's prostitution paid for your education and all the other nice stuff you've gotten. Those Toms didn't have a dime until Lillie died and left her grandson wealthy. They lived off you and Lillie's ill-gotten gains like roaches at a picnic."

Sister Betty's jaw dropped and her knees

started to shake. What was God trying to do to her? She was about to spiritually overdose on too much information.

"It don't matter to me none whether you accept the truth or not. You are still a fraud. You won't lift your congregation or community out of this economic mess because of your pride. You've done preached yourself into a corner of self-righteousness and you won't come out of it for your people's sake."

"How can you say that? I've just learned all this in the past hour."

"I can say it because you've said it. You don't wanna accept the trustee's so-called tainted money for God's business yet you are in God's business because of tainted money."

Cheyenne signaled for Sister Betty to help her from her seat. "I'm tired, so if you don't mind I'll accept your invitation to spend the night at your house. I'm ready to go as soon as you are. I can't wait to pass out in one of those fancy bedrooms."

Cheyenne yawned, then spoke as if the reverend weren't in the study. "Sister Betty, just remember to handle that hardheaded, self-righteous pastor of yours sitting over there. I don't cotton to nobody messing with the church whether it's from the outside or the inside, or whether I belong to it or not."

Sister Betty's mind raced as she asked the question that lingered on her and the pastor's minds. "Does anyone else around here know about Lillie Sinclair?"

"Bea 'Baby Doll' Blister probably does. She and I are the last of the really high-class players from the Charleston and D.C. days."

"Mother Bea Blister! Baby Doll?" Sister Betty thought she'd flatline right on the spot.

Reverend Tom sprang from his chair. "Why hasn't Bea said anything? Everyone knows she's done a little time before and that she is always scheming to get money."

"First of all, Bea can't say nothing that won't cause a lot of grief for others. Bea and I are cut from the same cloth. We've done our dirt, but we don't like aiding the Devil in attacking the church. In fact, Bea ran four of the most successful gambling houses in Charleston. Baby Doll and I know so much about some of those old hypocrite geezers. I betcha if we told them to give us their social security checks or we'd tell it, they wouldn't hesitate. They'd probably break a hip trying to rip it from their pockets."

"Father, have mercy, I don't know what

to do now," the reverend whispered as he looked toward the ceiling.

"Well, you'd better figure it out before Trustee Noel and that geriatric mafia arrives." There was a quick twitch to Sister Betty's face, then a puzzled look took over. It wasn't about to go away. Someone had turned the knob.

CHAPTER 22

"I didn't see the light on in here," Elder Batty Brick lied. "We just wanted to use the choir room to count up the receipts and discuss how the affair fared."

Elder Batty Brick and Brother Casanova crept quietly into the room. They would've walked harder, but stern looks from Bea and Sasha were a warning that something they didn't know about was going down. The truth was that he and Brother Casanova thought the room was unoccupied and were going to divvy up the tips and hush money they'd made.

As soon as the men walked to the center of the room, they heard Reverend Tom and female voices.

"Who's the pastor got in the office?" Brother Casanova adjusted his hearing aid and twitched his nose as though he could smell the sound. "One of them women is Sister Betty." He twitched his nose again and once more adjusted his hearing aid. "I'm not recognizing the other voice. It sounds like a white woman, though."

"Hush up, you old crabapple." Sasha pointed with her cane to the AC vent that went from the choir room into the study. She then laid her finger to her mouth to indicate that they shouldn't speak.

However, Bea gave up her own finger, the middle one, and fled from the room.

She raced the few feet to the office. The one-strap feature holding her dress together now held her back. Her breasts flopped around as though they didn't want to go wherever she was going. She felt her heart race, and her wide hips felt like flaps on an airplane slowing her down. She nearly bowled over Trustee Noel who'd just put his hand on the study's doorknob to enter.

Smashing the trustee against the door-frame, Bea burst into the study. She aimed her words at Cheyenne and let go. "Cheyenne Bigelow, how could ya just give up my business like that?" — Bea turned and pointed toward the reverend — "And to my pastor, of all people."

Cheyenne didn't answer right away. She motioned for the trustee to take one of the other seats. Just as she'd given him specifics about the food she'd yet to eat, Cheyenne had pointed to a seat over in the corner. Of course, Trustee Noel found it, plopped right down, and reached for that sprig of hair.

"Bea, everybody knows you been to prison, but I didn't think it'd do no harm if they knew how back in the day you was Bea 'Baby Doll' Blister. You set the standard for all the gambling houses in Charleston and there about." Cheyenne's face softened, "You didn't want none of these folk to know how successful you were as a business-woman?"

"She almost went bankrupt trying to run a daycare center." Sister Betty interrupted. "How could she be so successful at gambling and couldn't run a simple daycare?"

"Were them babies gamblin' in the day-care center?" Bea shot back at Sister Betty.

"Of course not, Bea," Sister Betty replied. "They were only babies."

"Well that's why it failed." Bea sucked her teeth and returned to her issue with Cheyenne. "I've spent the last half of my life try-ing to turn things around for me, and then you go and tell my business. You had no right to do that, Cheyenne."

"Bea, did you overhear everything I said?"

"No, I didn't. But I did hear ya mention my old street name, Baby Doll."

Reverend Tom thought it was a good time

212

to enter the conversation. After all, the horse was out of the barn so he might as well ride it. "Mother Bea, I understand you also knew my grandmother Lillie Sinclair."

"Yes sir, Pastor. I knew Lillie." A sign of struggle appeared as another wrinkle upon Bea's dark complexion. She wasn't quite sure where her pastor's questions were leading, so she turned and looked at Cheyenne for further instructions. Cheyenne smiled a little and Bea relaxed.

Reverend Tom clasped his hands together and moved his body so his chair swiveled. "Did you know Lillie when she supposedly sold herself as a prostitute?"

Bea's mouth clamped so tight the echo of her thick lips smacking together made the only sound. If she could've fled the room she would've. Instead, she stood in the middle of floor fidgeting. She didn't know what to say.

Bea turned away from her pastor's stare. With laser beam accuracy, she fixed her eyes on one of his many certificates, refusing to look away, and hoping no one saw her pain. Bea knew in her heart that Lillie Sinclair would never have stood for any of the mess her grandson had created for his church.

Bea suddenly pushed one of her fingers under her wig and straightened what didn't need straightening. What needed straightening was the truth. She wrestled with telling the reverend that Lillie paid tithes on the money she'd made on servicing men. In fact, most of the Charleston high life crowd paid tithes. They didn't go inside the church, but they cut anyone who said or did anything against it. She understood Cheyenne's position on a lot of matters. She just didn't like the way Cheyenne put her business out there.

Meanwhile, after Bea fled the choir room, Elder Batty Brick, Sasha, and Brother Casanova remained and listened with their ears pinned to the AC duct on the wall. It was their intention to snoop quietly.

Yet as soon as Elder Batty Brick overheard the reverend ask Bea whether she knew about Lillie Sinclair and he heard nothing from Bea, Elder Batty Brick reared back and boasted loudly, "Oh, Lillie was a fine ride. I should know . . ." By the time he put his hand over his big mouth the only thing he saved was a few teeth. Sasha punched him right in his grill.

Everyone in the study shut up. The only sound was that of Elder Batty Brick's confirmation coming from the choir room, followed by his scream. What they didn't know was Sasha had used her cane to whack

Elder Batty Brick in his big mouth.

Five minutes later, after they'd been caught snooping, Sasha and the men joined the others in the pastor's study. Sister Betty, Cheyenne, and Trustee Noel sat on one side of the desk, Bea, Sasha, and Brother Casanova sat on the other side with Reverend Tom seated in the middle. Elder Batty Brick stood near the door holding a rag over his bloody mouth. In case he needed to leave suddenly, he'd said.

The conversation continued after the reverend rebuked Sasha and the men for their un-Christian-like behavior. During the next half hour, the reverend learned that his grandmother Lillie was indeed quite popular. At least the way Elder Batty Brick and Brother Casanova bragged about her expertise. Of course, back then, they didn't know Jesus, but the way they expressed their appreciation for his grandmother was a bit too graphic for the reverend's taste. It appeared they hadn't come out of their throwback mood.

The only one, other than Sister Betty and Trustee Noel, who'd not contributed to Grandma Lillie's dubious occupation, was Sasha. *I'm beginning to have a bit more respect for Reverend Tom. He might have just enough hidden gangster genes to pull the church out of this mess. He just needs some prompting, that's all.*

"I don't know about the rest of you, but I'm tired. We got church in the morning in case y'all have forgotten." Sasha rose and turned to Trustee Noel. "Do you think I can catch a ride back with you and Sister Betty in your fancy car?" Sasha didn't wait for an answer before she turned and pointed her cane at Bea. "I'm too grown up to play with baby dolls."

Bea felt the temptation to set Sasha straight from her wig to her toenails, but she didn't. She glanced over at the reverend and, again, felt the pangs of guilt.

Elder Batty Brick offered to take Bea home. He knew too well there was no way Brother Casanova would take her.

CHAPTER 23

The throwback Seniors Prom had taken craziness and feuding to another level. By the time those Crossing Over Sanctuary seniors finished partying, drinking, and dancing their way through a modern day Egypt, there wasn't a tube of Bengay or a bottle of Geritol found around Pelzer. But the event was a cakewalk compared to what lay ahead.

Reverend Tom tossed and turned all night. The legacy of his grandmother Lillie Sinclair erased all he'd known to be true. Before Cheyenne's revelation, he'd been ready to toss aside what Bea told him about members of the congregation as gossip and hearsay. He tolerated to a small degree that not all were as saved as he. He couldn't do that any more.

Sunday morning arrived, bringing not a bit of rest for the weary. He pondered the vision he had when he'd fasted and prayed.

He recalled the beautiful woman who'd worn the ankle bracelet of a harlot and how she gave away her jewelry to the old woman. He remembered how young the old woman became when she received the gift of jewelry. It was as though she'd been reborn.

Stoking the fire in his fireplace, he looked into the flames and remembered the beautiful woman and the bright light that engulfed her body; the same light that had shone on the old man in rags who'd inherited the castle.

The crackling sound of the logs surrendering to the power of the fire caused the reverend to shake. As strong as he was he suddenly became weak as he remembered more of his vision. The young man in the preacher's robe had taken, not given, and the people fell before him, moaning as he touched them.

He'd nearly done that. He wanted all the support and long-suffering of his members, but he'd caused them pain in the process.

The reverend looked at the clock. There wasn't enough time for even a power nap. He stood and walked over to his desk. Fingering one of the red ribbon placeholders that protruded from his Bible, he started to open it up, but instead started to pray. "Jesus, I've fasted and I've prayed and my wall of Jericho has fallen on top of me. I'm too tired from beating my head against that wall. Whatever it is, even if it's about my grandmother, please make it plain. I'm too tired for parables this morning."

With time moving much faster than he did, the reverend showered and left for the morning service. He had no idea what he'd say or from which book he would bring the message. He wasn't even certain if there'd be a packed sanctuary since so many had attended the Seniors Prom the night before. He determined to press on anyhow. "Your will Lord; Your will and Your way . . ."

Reverend Tom, deep in thought, passed by his turnoff to the church. Since he needed to go down the road to make his U-turn he decided to drive past the Promised Land development. As he approached the development, he saw six men there. He slowed down and realized three of the six men were the Cheater Brothers.

They stood alongside several other men. All the men appeared to have large sheets of paper in their hands. The reverend didn't bother to stop. His fists pounded the steering wheel. "The Devil is a liar!" Those words had become his way of avoiding cussing. Lately, it hadn't worked as well as he'd liked.

Reverend Tom felt helpless as he realized the bank had already decided that he wouldn't make the Christmas deadline. No doubt, the news of declining Trustee Noel's generous offer had made the rounds. The Piece of Savings Bank had begun to proceed as though they'd already reclaimed the land.

Reverend Tom didn't realize how angry he'd become until a state trooper pulled him over.

Unfortunately for the reverend not only was he clocked at speeds of more than seventy miles per hour in the fifty-five zone, but the trooper turned out to be a member of Crossing Over Sanctuary. While he wrote out and handed the ticket to his pastor, he went further than issuing a warning along with it.

"Reverend Tom, right now I'm a man on his job and thank God I have one. But you, sir, have a chance to help your members who are struggling and you haven't. You might want to think faster about that and drive slower."

The trooper doffed his wide-brimmed hat and added, "You have a good day. It was only God's traveling mercies that prevented an accident or worse."

Reverend Tom didn't respond. He couldn't argue with the trooper. The trooper couldn't let him slide any more than the reverend did the trustee. Shoving the ticket into his topcoat pocket, he shook his head and muttered, "No sleep and now a speeding ticket." He was angry, yet on his way to preach, tired to the bone.

There was no sleep for the trustee either. For the past few hours, Trustee Noel lay in his small bed and shivered. The Soul Food Shanty's heater was broken again, producing nothing more than nerve-racking rattling sounds from a rusty radiator.

Between the heater's clanging and him learning of the reverend's grandmother's rather unconventional career choice, Freddie Noel had not slept a wink.

He tossed and turned. He was angry one moment and praying the next. The only break he caught was a silly grin that broke through when he realized his sudden infatuation with Sister Betty.

Since he didn't sleep much through the night, he rose and laid out another JCPenney unoriginal suit. He wanted to give Sister Betty a feast for her eyes. He chose a black, three-button pinstripe, a white shirt, and black and white tie with zigzag lines throughout. His spit-polished black Florsheim shoes had white flaps. The sales clerk

221

had promised he'd be the only one wearing them. *She'll like this one.*

As pleased as he was with his new sense of style, he couldn't push past his disappointment with Reverend Tom. Last night, before they'd all gone their separate ways everyone hugged or shook hands before departing. Everyone, including Bea and Sasha acted civil, but not he and the reverend. There was still that matter of the twenty-five million dollars and it shadowed their every move. "He's such a stubborn mule. He should've apologized last night as soon as he found out his grandmother's money was as tainted as he'd called mine."

Trustee Noel didn't realize how upset he was until he heard the words leave his mouth. It was no way to prepare for service and for that he was angry at the reverend, too.

The clock on Sister Betty's kitchen wall read five o'clock and there were hints of a bleak sunrise on the horizon. Neither she nor Cheyenne had slept a wink since they'd arrived back at Sister Betty's house. The women spent most of the night seated at the kitchen table. They snacked on Little Debbie cupcakes and tea while they chatted, waiting for someone who was due to

222

arrive in about another hour to drive Cheyenne to her home in Belton.

"I should be worn out. An old lady at my age should try and take better care of herself, but I can sleep on my way home," Cheyenne teased as she waited. "You, my dear Sister Betty, can sleep during the service. I doubt if Reverend Tom will wanna whoop and holler this morning."

Cheyenne sighed. "I know I wouldn't want to if I'd been hit like he was last night. But that uppity something had it coming. Lillie never wanted nothing but the best from and for him."

Just like the night before in the reverend's study, Sister Betty wanted to push back on Cheyenne's disrespectful remarks, but she didn't. Not only was Cheyenne a guest in her home, but the woman spoke close to what was on Sister Betty's mind.

She sipped slowly from her cup of hot cayenne pepper tea, as did Cheyenne with a cup of orange ginger tea. In between sips, as they waited for the car, they discussed last night's conversation inside the pastor's study.

"I probably should've told everything I know." Cheyenne took another sip of tea, then rested her hands on the table. Another second and her hands would've felt the hot tea that spurted from Sister Betty's mouth.

"Oh, I'm so sorry." Sister Betty poured more tea into her cup to replace what she'd spat out. She knew she had to speak up whether Cheyenne was a guest or not. "I don't know if I can take another word against my church or my pastor. I don't believe God is pleased with all this."

"You are probably right. I'm sorry. You know me; I'm just an old political drama queen." Cheyenne's apology accompanied a nervous laugh.

The conversation had taken another turn that neither woman wanted to visit. By the time the car service arrived it brought relief to both. They said their good-byes and promised to keep better in touch with one another. Cheyenne said she'd call once she arrived in Belton.

Sister Betty was exhausted. She felt a bit eerie and didn't know why, then realized she'd never called for her ride to take her to church. Brother Randy, one of the church's young deacons she'd hired as her on-call driver, had left earlier with Cheyenne. A glance at the clock showed that it was almost a quarter after seven. She dialed the reverend's home. *Maybe I can catch a ride with him.* After her third attempt at calling, she gave up. The first two times she thought he'd might've been in the shower. The last try meant either he was ignoring her or he actually wasn't home.

The camera inside the pastor's study scanned the sanctuary and the hallways. Reverend Tom pushed back in his chair and put his chin in the palm of his hand. It was almost time for the second service. While his fingers tapped out a rhythm on his desk, he surveyed the sanctuary and parking lot for the last time. There wasn't a lot of activity in either place. Whoever was coming apparently was already there. Of course, he suspected the seniors had partied way past their bedtimes and probably would've fallen asleep during the service had they come. However, packed sanctuary or not, he still had to preach the Word.

He bowed his head and whispered a prayer. "Holy Ghost, you bring the word."

The choir sang, announcements were made, and a missionary offering was held. Welcome was extended to all, first-time visitors in particular. The request for the members to stand was given, then the ushers, stoic as usual, escorted the reverend into the service. It was time to preach again.

Because it was the last Sunday of the month it was also Communion Sunday. As customary when he served the Last Supper the reverend dressed in all white. In front of the pulpit on a long narrow table draped entirely in white linen were the wine and wafers. He felt unqualified to serve them, but he'd have to deal with that later.

Rarely was church business done on Communion Sunday, but it was the last quarter. Later that afternoon, members would return for the business meeting.

The congregation appeared a bit restless, shuffling Bibles and feet from side to side as they awaited his text.

"Today, I am led by the Holy Ghost," the reverend explained as his fingers flipped through the large print Bible on the podium. "A lot has occurred here at Crossing Over Sanctuary and God is cleaning house." He pointed first at himself, then over the members. "None of us is complete unless God does the work. We're all a work in progress."

He hoped the Spirit was leading him because at that moment, he floundered for a text to bring it all together. Without giving another thought, he looked down at his Bible and felt unexpectedly light in his spirit. It was as if every burden he'd borne for the past twenty-four hours suddenly lifted off his shoulders. Within seconds, his lips began fluttering and his knees buckled slightly. He threw his head back, and as he slowly brought his head forward, his words were barely audible. They became unintelligible sounds of a language understood by God alone. Snippets found their way via the microphone into the ears of the congregation, but it was okay. He and the church knew the Holy Ghost had taken control. Sounds came and although he knew he'd begun to speak in tongues, he was surprised.

Reverend Tom and God had a heart-to-heart, spirit-to-spirit experience. The pastor's face glistened and suddenly from over in the corner where the deacons sat came more tongues and those met and agreed with the reverend's utterances.

Then it all died down and he began to read.

CHAPTER 24

"I will begin at Acts 10:14," the reverend announced. "If you have your swords — Bibles to those not familiar with that term — then please read along with me."

Sister Betty watched with interest and awe. She'd managed to get a ride and had arrived at the end of the missionary offering. She nodded at the two church mothers who had somehow managed to get to the service. She wasn't surprised when she didn't see either Bea or Sasha. She was almost relieved. She didn't feel like playing the role of spiritual probation officer with those two.

Trustee Noel sat with a few other men. The reverend's confidence caught him off guard. He figured after the reverend discovered his grandmother sold her body, he would've preached about the woman at the well or even the woman caught in the act of adultery. He certainly didn't expect him to preach from Acts, particularly since he seemed so embedded in church law without compromise. The trustee took a moment and looked toward where Sister Betty, Bea, and Sasha usually sat. He found only Sister Betty, her eyes fixated on the pulpit. He turned and did likewise.

Reverend Tom normally had one of the deacons read the text scripture but not that morning. He was God's general on a mission and if he needed his army, he'd call them, but at that moment, he fought alone.

"But Peter said, Not so, Lord; for I have never eaten anything that is common or unclean." The reverend stopped reading and ran his hand through his hair, although there was not a strand out of place. He was the only thing out of order. He withdrew a large handkerchief from his sleeve, wiped his brow and continued. "And the voice spake unto him again the second time, what God hath cleaned, that call not thou common."

He slowly closed his Bible and came down from the pulpit.

There was none of the usual enthusiasm or prodding from the congregation. No "amen," or "preach, pastor, preach." Even the men who, moments before, had confirmed the pastor speaking in tongues with a display of their own were silent.

Before the entire congregation, the pastor testified of his journey through his prayer and fast. He went from summation to testifying without interruption.

Reverend Tom ran the gamut. The words poured from him and he was helpless to leave out anything. He confessed how he thought he'd lost his mind when he wrestled with an angel. He connected the dots of his vision of the woman wearing the harlot's ankle bracelet. "And then I discovered my beloved grandmother, Lillie Sinclair, sold her body for money. That same money sent me to divinity school to preach God's word and the interest on that investment stands humbled before a tolerant congregation."

From across the sanctuary the reverend heard, "Tell it. God is the master builder," and "Let Him use you, pastor," and "Nasty money ain't always nasty." He had no idea from whom or from where exactly the encouragements came. He was in the zone that only those connected directly to the power of God experienced. Everything else became background noise.

When he'd told almost all he needed to reveal, he was exhausted. But he wasn't finished. Taking a deep breath, he returned to the pulpit.

He wiped his brow again and almost threw his body across the top of the podium. He allowed the congregation to rest for a moment along with him. Then he became irritated, but in a good way.

The reverend said to the congregation, "I know without a shadow of doubt that this morning on my way here, God led me to pass by the Promised Land. He wanted to give me a spiritual view of what stood in my way, and it was me. Yet also in my natural view, across the road from this church were the Cheater Brothers from the bank."

The reverend felt a sudden surge of power. His arm muscles rippled beneath his robe as his hands gripped both sides of the podium. He began to claw at the Plexiglas. He'd be a hypocrite if he said he wasn't upset.

In an instant, disapproving mumbling rang out across the sanctuary. "Don't let the enemy take you there." One of the deacons encouraged, "You know God fights your battles."

The reverend showed his agreement when he added in a raised voice, "As I said, I saw the Cheater Brothers along with some other men. I didn't stop to make introductions, but I believe they were the potential buyers." Pointing suddenly in the direction of

Trustee Noel and several other members of the Finance Committee, he added, "but I am also certain those brothers seated over there stand with me when I say that the news of Crossing Over Sanctuary losing the Promised Land is a bit premature."

The congregation was few in number that Sunday morning. However, they jumped to their feet and began to praise God. The way they shouted, bucked, whooped, and screamed was as though the Lord had descended and walked amongst them.

The organist stood. He pushed the hem of his choir robe to the back, raised one leg on the organ stool, and pounded the organ keys. He worked the choir and the worshippers into a frenzy.

There was no rest for the ushers that morning. They raced from one energetic congregant to another shoving, covering, fanning, and caressing those worshippers who'd fallen out like dominoes.

CHAPTER 25

The service had ended almost two hours ago and the reverend hadn't left the church. He'd debated whether to go home or stay until the business meeting.

Neither Elder Batty Brick nor Brother Leon Casanova had made it to the morning service. Without the full Finance Committee present the reverend met with Trustee Noel who'd seemingly latched onto Sister Betty and wasn't letting go.

"I cannot apologize enough," Reverend Tom told Trustee Noel. "You can believe I will make a public apology at the meeting this afternoon as well."

"There's no need for that Reverend Tom. Just you standing up there in front of the entire church and addressing me was good enough."

"Okay Moses and Joshua," Sister Betty interjected, "this is only one battle. We haven't won the war yet."

Reverend Tom and Trustee Noel gave Sister Betty a questioning look.

Reverend Tom asked, "Sister Betty, I just said that we will take the Promised Land. What do you mean we haven't won the war?"

"I'm talking about from here on. Taking the Promised Land is just one battle. Are you certain you can accept all this unrighteousness that is a part of your church?"

"Ma'am." Reverend Tom didn't want her to throw cold water on what he felt was his aha moment, but she had doused it completely. "I'm not quite sure I know what you mean."

She could see the effect her words had on him. She truly didn't want to see his glorious worship abruptly ended. He was a much better spirit when he was in the Spirit.

"What I'm asking is whether or not you can accept that perhaps there's more evil or tainted money floating around and supporting our church than you know about. What you do about it from this point on will probably depend on how much you can accept now. God has shone a light on something that had just as much to do with your pride as it did with the bad habits of your flock."

Trustee Noel in an earlier moment before he knew the reverend was going to accept his tithes might've just kept quiet. However, a lot had happened in the past twenty-four hours. He felt he had about twenty-five million reasons to say something. So he did.

"I say we table this for another time. The business meeting will start soon and we need to prepare." He spoke with a new confidence that wasn't lost on Sister Betty and the reverend. They quickly looked around to see if he were lipsynching someone else's words.

Reverend Tom pondered what the trustee added to the conversation. He found nothing useful nor would it explain Sister Betty's concern, but he said nothing. If he'd learned anything in the past weeks, it was that he needed to listen more and speak less.

Sister Betty leaned her head to the side and adjusted her Bible. She'd begun to admire the changes she saw in the trustee, but now wasn't the time for admiration. She needed to reset his clock right then and there.

"You were blessed when you won that Mega Lottery, were you not?" She turned and faced the trustee head-on. She turned her back to her pastor and didn't include him in the rebuke.

"Yes, I was very blessed." Trustee Noel tried to understand where she was going with her questions, but he couldn't.

"If you'd won twenty dollars in a scratch off and tithed two dollars would you have been just as happy giving?"

"Yes, I would. I always tithe ten percent of whatever I get. It's just that I wanted to tithe more than ten percent this time. I've not missed tithing from my social security, either. It's not like I haven't won money before . . ." He clamped his hand over his mouth and reached for that sprig of his. He realized where she'd led him and he'd stepped right into it.

Sister Betty smiled. She gotten what she needed from the trustee and hoped the reverend understood.

He did. He would never know where a blessing came from unless it was shown to be so.

He stood from behind his desk and walked over to one of the bookcases in his office. He took down four leather-bound books, each one representing a different milestone in the church's history since he became the pastor. He placed them on top of a stack of other books that included his personal Bible.

"When I prayed and fasted," the reverend began, "I asked God not to show me in parables, but to show me in a way that was undeniably Him."

"Be careful when you offer the Lord a challenge like that," Sister Betty said softly. "He won't and can't back down. He's not like man. He cannot lie." She walked to where the reverend stood and smiled.

"And He won't change His mind about His business, either." She placed a hand on the reverend's arm, and with the conviction of a seasoned woman of God, she added, "and sometimes when He throws back the covers, the sheets are dirty and in need of changing. But you still gotta sleep somewhere."

Trustee Noel saw Reverend Tom kiss Sister Betty on the cheek, then on the back of her hand. He wanted to say something about how inappropriate he thought of his pastor's action. He'd never had those feelings before. He wondered if he felt jealous after a cooked meal and a limo ride. He hoped not.

"I know what to do now," Reverend Tom announced as he looked at the security monitor. The members had begun arriving for the meeting. "Let's get ready for the business meeting."

He suggested that Sister Betty and Trustee Noel join hands and pray along with him. He asked God to continue guiding him and that he not make a complete fool of himself. He was as earnest in his last request as he'd been in the first.

By the time the three entered the sanctuary it was almost packed. More than fifteen auxiliaries came to the meeting with a lot to say.

Although not the entire Mothers Board made it to the meeting, somehow Bea and Sasha did. Not too far away Elder Batty Brick and Brother Casanova sat with other committee and board members.

Once the formalities were done — prayer, reading the minutes, and placing new business on the table — they got down to business.

Word about that morning service and the reverend's sudden change of heart had gotten around. However, most wanted to personally see and hear it.

Reverend Tom had changed from his preaching robe into his street clothes. The business meetings were very informal in dress. Anything from coveralls to Timberlands dotted the sanctuary. Three people at the meeting hadn't worn dungarees or something simple. Sister Betty and Trustee Noel stood out because they hadn't changed since coming to morning service. Alice "Grandma Puddin' " had thrown back a bit too much at the Throwback Seniors Prom. She'd shown up wearing a two-piece outfit with her belly peeking out. From a distance, her ugly stretch marks made it seem as though she'd worn corduroy.

Reverend Tom took his place at the podium and began the business meeting. "Many months ago, we all came together and agreed with the vision God gave me. We agreed that Pelzer was becoming like Egypt in the Bible with the economy dropping, young people leaving and our senior citizens barely eking out a living. We promised to tithe and we'd all get to the Promised Land. Since that time some of us have had to make some hard choices." He looked around before he asked, "Are we in agreement thus far?"

When no one disputed what he said the reverend continued. "There are a few members who are barely above the poverty level, so of course, their choices are very different."

He stepped down from the pulpit. It wasn't a time for him to look down across the sanctuary. He needed to meet his congregation on their level and some of their levels were dismal.

He stood by the first pew where some of his most senior or handicapped sat on pews.

Some came to the meeting with their health aides, but most had to do for themselves.

"We have some members, I've recently learned, that are at the point where my heart is broken for them. I'm told they usually make the hard choices that depend on whether its Alpo or Kibble and Bits that is on sale. They buy day-old bread. Some are dividing pills to make them last."

A sea of nods in agreement appeared, but no one said a word.

"Whatever price they paid for those things will set how much they can put toward the rent. Right now, they can eat or they can sleep, but its hell trying to do both. We cannot take away their hope."

"That's just nasty and you know that, too." Brother Casanova frowned and hissed, "Ain't none of us doing that bad! Who's robbing from their grocery store money to pay rent?"

As the harsh words left his mouth, Brother Casanova looked around the sanctuary. He saw Elder Brick cringe and shake his head in dismay. On another pew, he saw a young woman with three small children seated next to her like stair steps. The young woman with her shoulders lowered as though she'd already surrendered to her burden, removed brown framed bifocal glasses with double-thick lenses. She wiped away a tear that seemed bigger before she'd removed those thick lenses. Against the church rules, he saw the children nibbling hungrily on cookies from a napkin. They ate without dropping a crumb.

Then Brother Casanova looked over at Bea and Sasha. He saw how the two proud old women sat then with their bodies stiff in defiance, yet they wouldn't even lift their faces to meet his gaze.

"My God," Brother Casanova threw up his hands. "My God, I didn't know how blessed I am. I never thought it had come to this for some of our church family. Are we not our brother's keepers?"

Reverend Tom hung his head. No wonder the body of Christ was doing so badly. He was the head of the church and in worse shape because of pride.

The unexpected outburst from Brother Casanova emboldened the reverend. He had a long speech prepared, but it paled in comparison to the hurt that had surfaced. He'd asked God to show him not in parables, but in reality. God was doing just that and more.

Reverend Tom began to speak. "Some were here this morning and know my position on some of our current situations. For the benefit of those who weren't at the morning service, I'd like to reiterate.

"Over the past few weeks, a lot has happened. Satan has appeared at every turn and seems comfortable in bringing strife to Crossing Over Sanctuary. As I said earlier, I've prayed, fought, prayed some more, and fought some more. I don't know about you, but I want to start over again. Have we grown into a church that does not care or cannot take care of its own? What does it profit to gain the whole world and lose one's soul?"

He stopped speaking, turned, and walked to the middle of the chancel and stopped in front of a large high-back chair. The church called it the VIP throne where visiting dignitaries often sat. He placed his hand on the back of the chair.

"This afternoon, we're gonna try something different, an experiment. We're putting Satan on notice and we're gonna reason together as though Jesus himself was the moderator, sitting right here listening and watching."

No one said a word. They couldn't. He'd come from as far left field as they'd ever seen. Moreover, before they could grasp what he meant, the reverend pulled a purple strip of material from his pocket and wrapped it around the back of the chair. He placed a Bible on the seat.

Hardly a person attending that business meeting didn't think they needed to call an intervention for their pastor. However, the only ones bold enough to say so were Bea and Sasha.

"I do believe he done gone too far now." Bea moved closer to Sasha, pretending to straighten the blond wig she'd worn especially for the business meeting, thinking it made her stand out more when she had something to say. It did.

Bea leaned over and whispered loudly to Sasha, "I ain't got no minutes left on my cell phone. Can you call that nut doctor that treats your family?"

Before Sasha could respond, the reverend rebuked Bea. "Mother Blister, we're trying to have the meeting. When the floor is open then you can voice any concerns you have."

"Harrumph." Sasha moved away from Bea. She looked around at the other members to see if any agreed that her family needed a nut doctor.

With eyes straight ahead and on the reverend, the entire congregation could've won an Oscar. Everyone knew Sasha and her entire Hellraiser clan needed the services of not only a nut doctor, but an exorcist, too.

When he finished decorating the chair Reverend Tom continued. "We are supposed to love each other as Christ loved the church. Christmas is right around the corner and we're supposed to celebrate His birth. Yet, we're backbiting and acting a fool and there's not a one of us who can claim ownership of salvation more than another, and yet we do. Me especially."

Reverend Tom walked over and stood in front of the pulpit. "Y'all just remember that Jesus is listening and watching from that empty chair."

CHAPTER 26

The bickering began as soon as the reverend opened the floor to the minds and hearts of the congregation.

"Why in the world would he put Jesus in a chair?" The question came at the reverend in various ways, but it added up to the same thing.

"I know this is a bit unusual," he told them. "In divinity school we used an exercise where we place Jesus in an empty seat. We wouldn't judge. We acknowledged that Jesus would do that. However, we had to tell the entire truth. After all, not only do we serve God in spirit and in truth, but as I said, He is watching us from that empty seat."

The church erupted. The reverend had given his congregation an early Christmas present. Only the members of the church attended the business meeting, so they dispensed with protocol and manners.

Things got ugly quick. Fights almost broke out as they jockeyed for space at the microphone. It was a miracle the reverend sat down without pain because they ripped him a new one before his butt hit the cushion. Every so often, they nodded at that empty VIP chair for Jesus' approval.

It didn't matter that they knew the reverend would now accept the twenty-five million dollars from Trustee Noel. Reverend Tom had been a snob in their minds for almost eight years, and they were going to let him know it.

The members gave the reverend more than an earful. They laid him out about everything. They griped about his selfishness toward the Promised Land project, not allowing them to sell tickets at the door when they held functions, and not taking a wife to share his wonderful life.

When they finished with him, Jesus probably hadn't seen that much hell since He snatched the keys from Hades early on Resurrection Sunday. They forgot they were supposed to reveal their grievances toward one another, but a man who'd turned down twenty-five million dollars deserved their full attention and wrath.

For a church that had not gotten down to the business of holding a business meeting the members were exhausted. It was the perfect opportunity for BS to start. And it did.

Sasha sashayed up to the microphone. She stood on her toes and spoke her piece as if Jesus watched everyone but her.

"It's good that you've promised to stop getting in the way of progress, but I still want to know how you managed to mess up my one hundred forty dollars and twenty-six cents."

Reverend Tom had had enough from Sasha. Without hesitating, he reached into his pocket and took out his wallet. He counted out the exact amount Sasha had complained about including the twenty-six cents. It took all the Christianity he had not to shove it in her face. He told her politely, speaking into the microphone for all to hear, "Mother Pray Onn, on behalf of Crossing Over Sanctuary church I am refunding your tithe for the year. I pray that God increases it and your faith. I am sure that without your tithe, whether we had Trustee Noel's millions or not, the church would survive."

Sasha was beyond embarrassed. She stood with her cane handle dangling from her tiny wrist, and while she counted the money he'd returned, including the twenty-six pennies, she threw Bea under the bus.

"And Bea wants to know why, when they turned off her lights, the church didn't come to her aid? You waited until the electric company threatened to turn off the street lights in front of her building before y'all gave her a dime."

Bea didn't mean to snatch off that blonde wig she had pinned under her wide-brimmed purple hat, but she did. With the wig in her chubby paw, she raced to the microphone and took a swing at Sasha with it. "I tole ya not to open ya big mouth about my business, didn't I?"

Bea swung and Sasha ducked. The two old women played the game of cat and mouse until they were exhausted and plopped down on the closest pew. Ushers reluctantly raced over and gave each a sip of water and a Martin Luther King fan before retreating to their posts.

Reverend Tom looked toward Sister Betty. She had her head down, no doubt praying. He looked toward the Church Board and the Finance Committee who stared back at him as though they'd just dipped their hands in a washbowl and he was brand new again.

All of that went down while the invisible Jesus watched from the high-backed VIP chair.

The photograph albums the reverend brought from his study went unopened. He'd meant to show the church how far they'd come from the time he'd taken over. As much as he'd fasted and prayed, he'd somehow managed to bring it all back to himself. From what he gathered from the membership, they'd achieved it in spite of him and most of it by means he strongly disapproved.

The sanity returned once the meeting turned to real church business. Personalities were set aside and with the probable influx of monies from not only Trustee Noel, who'd kept quiet during the melee, things became almost normal.

Reverend Tom wisely stepped aside and allowed the auxiliaries to make their reports.

Surprisingly the Seniors Prom almost tripled the initial five hundred dollar investment. Bea's handwritten T-shirts sold out completely and she had orders for almost five hundred more.

Sasha, however, didn't report how much she made from photographs that somehow never made it into their Seniors Prom book. Judging from the calm demeanor of the Mothers and Deacon Boards, apparently she'd made a killing.

No one was more surprised than Reverend

Tom when Sister Betty stepped forward. She didn't belong to any particular auxiliary for good reason: she preferred to remain an alternate. Too much drama and too little progress, she'd always said. But that afternoon, she had something to say, so everyone hushed.

"First of all," Sister Betty started, "I thought I'd be somewhat embarrassed by all that's been revealed today."

She turned toward her pastor and pointed. "I've never heard of no one whoring in my family and God using the funds to bring about some good, but if the pastor ain't embarrassed, neither am I."

Laughter rang out, not too loud at first, but it quickly grew into a roar. It might've been to take away the sting or the stench of embarrassment for the reverend or because of Sister Betty's quirky way of saying what needed saying.

"It's almost time to bring this meeting to a close, but some of what needs revealing is still hidden. I know because my left knee feels like a bowling ball dropped on it, so y'all know God done showed and told me something. Please don't let me hafta tell your business." Sister Betty pointed toward the high-back VIP chair. "Jesus is waiting and He may have an eternity to wait on you, but I don't."

"Oh Lord, please forgive me." The request came from one of the young men who sang tenor in the choir. Standing tall with a body built for tackling, he yelled out, "Pastor, when you spoke this morning from Acts ten, fourteen, and fifteen, I played the Big Four after service."

"Was it your first time?" Sister Betty asked slowly.

"No ma'am. I've been playing the sermon numbers since I joined the church five years ago. I used most of it when I donated the new choir robes two years ago. I promise you I will not ever do it again."

And that's when applause rang out over the sanctuary and the reverend made a mental note to find another way of presenting his text.

Sister Betty might as well have sprinkled conviction dust across the sanctuary. Testimonies of ill-gotten gains and their contribution to the church began with the tenor and didn't stop until someone standing by the exit had their say.

The reverend thought it only pertained to the improvements he'd been aware of in his photograph book. He wasn't even close.

Members confessed bartering for the hymnals to a few kickbacks on the combined grape juice and wafer sets. Even the new aluminum eight-eye Deluxe Chef's range in the church's kitchen had fallen off a truck, although no one explained how it fell off a truck without a report being made.

When the reverend got over his shock, he asked, "Why didn't I know about this?"

Elder Batty Brick spoke for the entire membership. "Because you never asked. You always praised God for the increase and never determined how it got increased. We were always in the news about what good we were doing so we just kept doing bad and asking for forgiveness."

The reverend felt as though he were not only a failure as a pastor, but that he was back to square one. "So, if I take the twenty-five million then I have to believe it's what God wants because of what God showed Peter on that roof."

And that's when a few of the folks who would never have been convinced Jesus sat in the high-backed VIP chair took out their dream interpretation books. They flipped the pages and looked up the word *roof* and its numerical meaning.

Sister Betty hadn't moved too far from the podium when she sat down to let the members have their say. Seeing the power-less look on the reverend's face, she returned to the podium.

"You know some of y'all make my teeth itch." She made a clicking sound with her partials, not only to show her disgust, but also to ensure the fit was still tight. Then she held up her Bible.

"This is your roadmap. This is how God speaks to us. I know y'all have read the same scripture or verse many times and it meant something different each time. Why did it hit you differently? It was because you had different needs."

She turned and pointed at the high-back VIP chair. "We can go back and forth till the Lord comes off that chair 'cause some of y'alls minds won't ever change and some change all the time. Just remember that when Moses led God's hardheaded children to that Promise Land, he wasn't gone but for a minute to talk to God like the reverend did on his recent fast and prayer. When Moses came back, they had lost their minds, much like y'all have. They melted down gold and such, even made idols that God told them were a no-no. And yet, God kept his promise and they went on to the Promised Land."

The eyes of the congregation didn't even blink while Sister Betty spoke. They swung between Sister Betty and the invisible Jesus in the high-back VIP chair.

"We know Moses, because he was disobedient, didn't make it to the Promise Land. He remained behind and only God could find him. One thing is now clear. Those thoughts Reverend Tom once had thinking he's righteous or better than y'all are what's left behind, too. He's brought a better insight into God's leading as we go to the Promised Land across the road."

Applause and amens went up. Reverend Tom sat farther back onto his seat and smiled. Almost everyone came onboard with Sister Betty's explanation.

But Bea wasn't that convinced. "So, are you sayin' that we can gamble whenever we want to and God's okay with it?"

Folks leaned forward in their seats. Most had agreed with Sister Betty's reasoning on how God sometimes blessed when it seemed that He shouldn't. But Bea's question merited an answer from Sister Betty.

"No, Bea, I am not. I was using the story of Moses leading God's people to the Promise Land as a metaphor for our situation."

Bea began to claw at that blond wig that she had put back on her big head. Whether she should show more ignorance than normal became her dilemma. She'd already put in her numbers for that day and wanted God's approval. "I don't know what a met a fore is, but I don't want it for my situation."

"Okay, Bea. Let me make it plain for you. Only the new generation of God's people made it to the Promised Land. All those gripers and idolaters didn't."

"So, Trustee Noel gets to go to the Promised Land even after he's been gambling, but I can't go?"

Things crumbled so fast that the reverend, Sister Betty, nor perhaps their invisible Jesus could've prevented it.

Trustee Noel jumped to his feet. He was so mad at Bea for creating what he'd decided was a mess that he blurted, "I played the numbers that you gave to Sister Betty on a piece of paper. I didn't always gamble like you do."

Every head in the sanctuary swung in Sister Betty's direction. Whatever chances Trustee Noel thought he had with Sister Betty, he'd just erased. He'd turned her into a numbers runner.

Trustee Noel explained as best he could Sister Betty's limited role in how he came into possession of Bea's paper with her numbers. When he saw her nod her approval, he felt better and certainly safer.

But Bea had enough of "met a-for" and

"randomly selected numbers." She felt she was in for a cut and if the trustee didn't fork over her money she would cut him.

While the trustee wrote out a check to Bea for money she didn't deserve, the reverend stood and went to the high-back VIP chair. His experiment had failed miserably. There weren't enough spiritually minded to go along with his unconventional experiment. With tears in his eyes, he apologized to Jesus for the absurdity of the whole matter.

Night fell before all the church business concluded. However, in the end they'd all come together and celebrated the idea that Crossing Over Sanctuary was on their way to the Promised Land.

CHAPTER 27

During the week after the business meeting news of the church's resurrection spread. They were going to the Promised Land unless something crazier than usual happened.

During the first week of December the cold should've kept folks in their homes. However, when the doors to the church opened that next Sunday members and visitors poured inside. Without a "Welcome to Crossing Over Sanctuary" greeting from the ushers they hurried to find a seat wherever they could.

Ushers raced to open the upstairs overflow sections. It still wasn't enough room and they had to place chairs in the aisles alongside the pews. It was the first time in the church's history where the Mothers, Deacons, Trustees, and Church boards shared pews. They didn't have a choice.

While the service formalities took place in the sanctuary, Reverend Tom remained inside his study. For the umpteenth time he and the trustee were going over their plans for presenting once more the twenty-five million dollar check and all it represented.

Reverend Tom looked more rested than he had in weeks, and almost ten years younger. God had not only restored his faith, but his vitality and it showed in the new red, white, and gold robe presented by the Pastor's Aid Committee. It was their early Christmas gift and he didn't question how they could afford it.

Trustee Noel, however, was a completely different matter. While they reviewed their plan, he happened to look in a mirror and saw his reflection. A big grin appeared upon his face.

After last week's church business meeting, he'd shopped again. In truth, he had come to the point where he just loved to shop. An outfit from JCPenney, instead of off the rack at the Salvation Army, was a come up. Unfortunately, the store's tailor hadn't been available so no alterations were done. He actually looked like the scarecrow from *The Wiz* in his ill-fitting suit, especially with that sprig of white hair spouting from the top of his head.

One of the ushers knocked on the study door and told them it was time to go to the sanctuary. Once they arrived, the trustee went ahead and found his seat reserved near the pulpit and the reverend was led inside a few moments later.

Reverend Tom preached until he had to come out of his new robe. His hair was a mess, huge round circles of sweat appeared under his armpits, and his voice grew hoarse. By the time he finished just about everyone in the sanctuary looked as messed up as he did. Everyone was on one accord with praise.

Then it was showtime for real. The reverend wanted the dedication to go a certain way, and the church had agreed to it.

The trustee stood. His skinny chest supposedly pushed out but it was too skinny to tell. With his annoying, silly grin still plastered on his face, he spoke.

"First of all, I want to give honor to God." Trustee Noel needed to get that part of his speech out of the way. He knew that any good church-going Christian would never start without that customary churchy-type acknowledgment.

"God has been good to me no matter how often I've felt my fellow man might not have been" — he let that little admonishment settle over the church — "but I love Crossing Over Sanctuary and I want to help."

By that time, the reverend had begun to move toward the trustee. In his mind, the trustee hadn't kept to the script since they'd discussed not bringing up old wounds. Reverend Tom wasn't but a few feet away when Trustee Noel sped up his speech.

"And so with great humility, I want to give a special offering. I am, once again, giving the church a check for twenty-five million dollars." He raised the envelope above his head, then walked over and handed it to the reverend.

There wasn't another sound heard throughout the sanctuary until Reverend Tom accepted the envelope from Trustee Noel's outstretched hand.

Sister Betty switched her Bible from one hand to the other as she wrestled with the scene unfolding in front of the pulpit. She had a proud look upon her face as though she witnessed her man performing a heroic deed. "Lord, help me," she murmured. "I don't wanna man. Please take this feeling away."

While Sister Betty sat a few pews away praying, the drama continued to unfold at the podium.

When the reverend took the envelope from his hand, Trustee Noel felt a flood of relief run through his body. His new personality had him as perplexed as those around him. He'd prayed for holy boldness. Perhaps he should've joined a Toastmasters speech class instead.

"I'm just going to sit down and let the pastor tell the church what I've done. He can do it better than me."

It became quiet as if another offering was requested.

As the reverend held up the envelope his eyes grew large. It was really happening. "I dedicate this tithe offering to God as the priests did in the Old Testament. We won't burn these twenty-five million dollars, but we give it as instructed by the Lord for the Promised Land."

Trustee Noel broke into some kind of awkward movement that could only be his version of a shout. "Hallelujah, praise Gawd!"

Of course, people started popping up all over the sanctuary. The shout-fest reignited and no one was happier than Bea Blister.

She'd been praising God for days once the trustee's check for five thousand dollars cleared. Bea jumped up off her pew seat, stopping just long enough to backhand Sasha on purpose. With her hunched back sticking out Bea used it to smack the faces of those still seated as she inched her way out of the pew. Bea's arms started flailing. No usher was crazy enough to mess with Mother Bea Blister when she was in the spirit or acted something akin to being possessed.

Of course, Sasha was in a different sort of pain, humiliated again by Bea. She had two reasons to shout. She wasn't about to let Bea get away with slapping her, then out-shouting her, too, so she jerked and shook as if lightning had struck her as she fake-danced her way over to Bea's side. Once she got there, she took the tip of her cane and jabbed Bea's pinky toe.

"Oh Jesus, Father!" Bea squealed, "Jesus, Jesus, oh Jesus!"

"Hallelujah Jesus, please touch this old nasty sinner." Sasha wiped the side of her eye as though there'd been a tear. She then wiggled her tiny hips; that signature move when she thought she'd had the last word on a matter. Hopping around as if praise came in an IV bottle and was hooked up to her, she joined the other Mothers who'd started shouting again.

Normally Sister Betty would've joined in. She always liked to see the Mothers of the church bring the praise. That time she decided she'd just praise God in her heart.

Visitors who'd come for a show that morning got their offering's worth.

CHAPTER 28

At exactly one minute after nine o'clock on Monday morning, December 27, Reverend Tom, Trustee Noel, and Sister Betty exited the reverend's car. They smiled and strolled into the Piece of Savings Bank. The closing for the Promised Land option was all but sealed and delivered.

All three of the Cheater Brothers, Ted, Skimp, and Slump, sat at a long table in the conference room. Seated with the brothers were their attorney and other closing personnel. The church's attorney, Sister Lizzie Hellraiser, dressed in high-neck blouse and fire-engine red power suit, sat across the table, facing the bankers. The forty-year-old niece of Mother Pray Onn was a fierce legal giant. She was expensive, but she'd beaten the infamous Gloria Allblack in a landmark case against the Family Penny Store. She earned every dollar.

One hand, with long, black polished nails,

strummed on a yellow lined notepad. The other fingered the cord attached to the frame of her glasses.

Sister Betty wasn't part of the Finance Committee and she certainly wasn't there to sign papers. Her role was to pray, and pray she did. She pled the blood on every one of those Cheater Brothers and the demons dressed in business suits seated beside them. With all the faith she and the others possessed, the truth was that none would be at ease until the papers were signed and processed.

Everything went according to plan. The closing didn't take long because the attorneys had worked out all concerns, and only signatures were needed. The Cheater Brothers grinned through the whole thing. As they'd put it, "We win no matter how it goes down." They had the church's money for the Promised Land and the trustee's remaining funds on deposit. They had no complaints.

Reverend Tom thanked his attorney and along with the trustee and Sister Betty was about to leave when the three Cheaters swooped down upon them. The men appeared sullen and he couldn't quite figure out why. When he happened to look at Sister Lizzie, she smiled and so did Sister Betty and Trustee Noel.

"You shouldn't do this," Ted Cheater said directly to Reverend Tom. "You are their pastor. They will listen to you."

The two other Cheater brothers voiced their concerns as well, mirroring their brother's.

"I have no idea what you are talking about." Reverend Tom wanted to leave so they could plan for the ribbon cutting ceremony. He didn't have time for games.

"You can stop them from withdrawing their monies. You have to do that!" The order came from Skimp Cheater.

That's when the reverend learned how seriously his members wanted to go to that Promised Land. They'd gathered to drown Pharaoh's bank army.

While the Promised Land closing went on in the conference room, his members stood in the teller lines closing their accounts. By the time the Cheater Brothers found out what happened the only one left in line was Sasha, and she wanted her money in a hurry. Of course, Reverend Tom, Sister Betty, and Trustee Noel didn't want it rumored that they hadn't participated. For the next thirty minutes the three, along with Sister Lizzie overseeing the transactions, withdrew their vast savings, IRAs, and any other monies available connected to that bank, then closed the accounts.

The Cheater Brothers were so outdone they ignored the chiming of the clock that alerted them to check the Wall Street status. That had never happened before. They realized once the news got out they'd be the laughingstock of the banking industry. One look at the impish grin on the overly qualified Sister Lizzie Hellraiser's face told them she'd make sure it was known.

CHAPTER 29

Cuttin' the Ribbon

Folks didn't know what was more newsworthy. Was it that the weather in Pelzer the Tuesday after Christmas was in the fifties? Or was it as most people believed, Crossing Over Sanctuary had made it to its Promised Land?

Local and out of state news reporters from television and radio covered the dedication. The media's arrival became fodder for some of the "showed up without invitation" self-appointed and self-righteous gospel queens and kings.

Those men and women's careers had long expired in the gospel world, but they still knew how to entertain. Folks doubled over with laughter as they watched the stampede to compete for face time in front of cameras that were pointed elsewhere. The competitors shoved decorum aside and tripped over their long flowing furs and walking sticks.

The reverend and congregation walked in and around the structures, those already built as well as those in progress.

The camera caught him weeping as he explained the battle to get to the Promised Land. He cried again when he read the letter from President Barack Obama congratulating him and the church for their dedication to community service. There was even a separate letter from the president encouraging Trustee Noel *". . . to keep exhibiting the spirit that makes America great."* It was basic enough for any recipient to read into it what they wanted.

The Cheater Brothers wept, too, but they wouldn't explain why they did. They didn't have to once the camera turned toward Sister Lizzie Hellraiser. She used all her legal skills to waterboard them with their sinful ways. When she finished with the *here to fores* and other legal jargon there wouldn't be a single threat of a lawsuit to follow.

If there was one wrinkle in the ceremony or the walkabout, Bea and Sasha caused it. It happened when the reverend showed the new senior apartment building and health care center that were in progress. The apartment building would have ten floors and each floor would hold ten apartments. The waiting list was already full and, sadly, some would have to look elsewhere. No one who'd filled out an application knew whether it'd been accepted or not, yet Bea and Sasha began to argue how they wouldn't want to live next door to each other.

"I'm Mother Sasha Pray Onn, the President of the Mothers Board," Sasha said into the camera. "I wouldn't live in the same building with She-Rilla if it was free of charge," she told one of the news reporters as she pointed at Bea.

Of course, Bea took offense. She grabbed the microphone from the reporter and barked, "I'm Mother Bea 'Baby Doll' Blister, Vice President of the Mothers Board. I want ya to know that Sasha Serpent Pray Onn is one nasty ole heffa. I wouldn't want her living in my building. She don't even keep a clean house."

Sasha took a bigger offense and snatched the microphone from Bea's hands. She turned and told the news reporter and the entire television viewing audience as she pointed to Bea, "She-Rilla don't know what she's talking about. I let my flies out every day for exercise. She can't claim to do the same for hers!"

"There you have it," the television reporter

270

said to the camera once he caught the microphone Sasha threw at him. "Church mothers gone wild."

The reverend quickly distanced the church affiliation from BS and proceeded with the ceremony. In about forty-five minutes, it was over. The journey to the Promised Land, all the gratuitous speeches, the keys, and the Pelzer proclamation handed to the reverend were finished. They held hands, prayed, sang, and then went their separate ways.

It was Trustee Noel's idea that later the Reverend and Sister Betty meet him at Porky's Soul Food Shanty to celebrate. He'd already invited a few others and informed Porky that he was bringing business his way. He didn't want to disappoint his landlord.

Against their better judgment, Sister Betty and the reverend gave in to the trustee, and agreed to meet him there about seven o'clock.

Several hours later, inside the Soul Food Shanty, the blue, white, green, and yellow Christmas lights hung with most of the small bulbs missing. A huge wreath with missing pinecones dangled from a nail on the front door. The wreath covered the latest egg launch by some unhappy patron. Christmas had come and gone, but even when it wasn't a holiday, business was slow.

Porky was up to his elbows in drama. He tried hard to convince the usual small group of loiterers to leave, but it was customary for the underprivileged to gather there. Most of them stopped by after work. Some had already spent their paychecks between the job and the bus stop. They came to Porky's to fill up on free helpings of false machismo, watered down non-alcoholic beverages, and pork rinds. With nothing to do and no money to spend, they spent time vigorously debating the same subject they had for weeks: the stupidity of Porky's now famous tenant, Trustee Freddie Noel.

"Why in the world would that man win millions of dollars and still stay in this ratty roach hellhole?" The question came from a young man who still had a WILL WORK FOR A SAMMICH sign hanging about his neck. To add insult to injury, Porky stood less than five feet away and heard it all. Before Porky could answer or produce a weapon, someone took up the debate.

Old man Sheffy was an elderly white wino and a longtime freeloader at Porky's place. He had teeth so yellow and sharp they looked like a gold serrated dagger between his puffy pink lips. He always had something to say even if he had to cut short whatever he was doing in the bathroom to say it. His pants were half down and he had toilet paper trailing from behind.

"I always thought that trustee was a damn fool and now I know he is one for certain." That said, Sheffy took his place on his regular stool without pulling up his pants.

In their delusions, everybody in the place excelled in economics, but none had a dime to show for it. They held hands, with the exception of Sheffy, whose hand no one wanted to touch, and sang Christmas carols and tried to recall the lyrics for rapper Kurtis Blow's "Those Are the Breaks."

While the inmates downstairs in the Shanty asylum talked about Trustee Noel, he began getting dressed upstairs. Every item he picked out had a *"What will Sister Betty think"* thought behind it.

If JCPenney didn't make it through the economic downward spiral, it wasn't because he hadn't done his part to help them.

Without benefit of any church fashion counsel, the trustee laid out a mixture of the old, the new, and several oh-hell-no outfits. Of course, he ended up choosing the latter.

Against his better judgment, but because

he wanted everyone to get along for the sake of the Promised Land, he'd told Porky to let the other customers remain. The way he figured, the church should never let things get out of hand again. There'd been too much blame leveled and even if they had cut the ribbon, they needed to start anew. Including Porky's destitute patrons was a good PR move.

After they'd promised to meet Trustee Noel at the Soul Food Shanty, Reverend Tom and Sister Betty thought of every excuse they could not to go. It wasn't just because of its nasty cuisine, but because something crazy always happened there. When they couldn't come up with a good excuse, they left to join the trustee.

He had invited others as well. Elder Batty Brick was one.

Although Elder Batty Brick had promised to keep the celebration a secret, he didn't. Ever since Bea cashed that check for the five thousand dollars and made him a red velvet cake, she gave him more power than any blue pill ever could. He refused to leave her side and was at Bea's whim. So of course, when he set off for the Soul Food Shanty, he had Bea along.

Brother Casanova had an invite from the

trustee as well. Unfortunately, on his way he ran into Sasha at the grocery store.

He felt bad when she complained about how the economy treated her like an unwanted stepchild. "I can't even buy this package of moldy cheese," she said, pointing to a wedge of blue cheese.

When Brother Casanova turned down the volume on his hearing aid and tried to escape down the canned food aisle, Sasha blocked his way and declared loudly, "Lord, I don't know what else to do. I'm trying to hold on to my one hundred and forty dollars and twenty-six cents tithes refund a little longer. I can't even afford a bus back home."

With people looking at him and shaking their heads as if he was the cheapskate, he offered her a lift. He hadn't intended to take her to the Shanty, but she'd badgered him into stopping at Mickey D's, then complained about the cost of a Happy Meal, so he caved in.

Trustee Noel wanted to keep the celebration intimate. There was a slight chance he might be alone with Sister Betty, so he paid Porky to let him rent the Shanty's back room. It was a room where Porky used to store his extra goods, but he hadn't served anything good since 1999 so it had gone unoccupied.

Porky hurried and gave a couple dollars to two of his loiterers to clean up the place. The young man willing to work for a sammich grabbed the money and started cleaning. In a short time he'd removed two cans of hardened paint, five or six occupied mousetraps, ran a damp mop over the floor, and used a half-dry rag over the fixtures.

Ole man Sheffy stood around with his pants still close to the ground and pointed. He picked his nose, then used that same finger to point to the things he thought hurt the décor and ambiance. "Just make sure you remove the table and chairs," Sheffy ordered. "They can sit Japanese-style on those old pieces of cardboard. That's the way we do it back in the alley."

When it was finished, the two men had the nerve to charge Porky extra to avoid filing for Worker's Compensation. Neither man had lifted anything beyond an elbow and a wine bottle for years and claimed they'd hurt their back muscles.

As for the menu for the evening, Porky offered to cook. When Trustee Noel reminded him that he wanted something particular, Porky reminded the trustee that he didn't cook particular and wouldn't know where to buy it or how to clean it. It was all last minute, but the trustee managed to get in touch with Alice "Grandma Puddin' " who said she'd handle it. Of course, he had to pay extra because she was tired from the renewed interest in her old stripper occupation since the Seniors Prom.

Everything was ready for the celebration. After that night in Pelzer, the Christmas season would never be the same. Even Old Satan threw more coal on the fire, popped some popcorn, gathered his demons, and looked up to watch.

In the meantime, Trustee Noel was in his room dancing and twirling that hair sprig. Nothing could erase the grin from his face while he sang his favorite Little Richard line, "Good Golly Miss Molly, sure love to ball."

CHAPTER 30

Reverend Tom and Sister Betty could barely find a parking spot. Every square inch on the block that surrounded the Soul Food Shanty was taken. The Christmas holiday weather was unseasonably mild and warm, causing a great deal of slush and mud. All they had to do was follow the footprints that led to the Shanty's front door.

If Sister Betty thought the seniors had rocked that prom the other week, she was in for a big surprise. They'd been amateurs.

She and the reverend's jaws dropped when Bea met them at the door. With "I saw Mommy kissing Santa Claus" blasting in the background, Bea sashayed over. She wore a halo of mistletoe that sat upon a wing-tipped, mauve-colored wig. Her hump was hidden under a fuchsia and black fur-trimmed gown. She wore a pair of stiletto heel boots she'd had cut down into flip-flops. She was a hot mess, but she felt good because there was money left over from her five thousand dollars.

"Come on in here and take a load off ya selves," Bea said. "I'm helping out with the celebration."

Bea was about to say something more when Elder Batty Brick's husky voice called out to her. "Bea, come back over here. Bring a slice of that red velvet cake and meet me in the back."

"I'm sorry, I can't stay and chat. My new man is calling me." Bea turned and with her back arched a little more than usual, she seemed to float to where Elder Batty Brick sat waiting.

Reverend Tom's voice finally returned about the same time as Sister Betty's. They looked at one another, each wanting to say something, but even with a voice, they couldn't.

The reverend slipped out of his coat and helped Sister Betty out of hers as they looked around.

Folks from all over Pelzer had squeezed into the Shanty. The Trustee's private celebration had turned into a public party. Apparently, Trustee Noel thought he owed a celebration, as well, to old man Sheffy and the other less fortunate who'd been a part of his life for so long.

The reverend and Sister Betty understood the unconventional guest list, and admired the trustee for his ability to remain humble.

Sister Betty, as usual, hadn't come prepared to partake in such a lavish celebration. She thought she'd shake it up a bit by wearing a gray and white long skirt and top. The only thing she had in common with some of the other guests was that she was wearing a wig, too.

The reverend, on the other hand, fit in just fine. After being stuffed into his robe most of the day for the ribbon cutting celebration, he was wearing a stylish, dark blue jogging suit. Some of the other men had dressed informally, except they hadn't changed clothes in weeks. The smell and wrinkles confirmed it.

Reverend Tom and Sister Betty decided to go with the flow until they spotted Brother Casanova. He kept moving around with Sasha almost tied to his hip. They laughed as poor Brother Casanova tried to shake her off his leg as though she were a piece of lint, or a small puppy in heat.

Finally, their host came downstairs. Trustee Noel wore a beige golf cap and a casual three-piece chocolate brown suit with the vest unbuttoned. Under the vest he wore a white muscle shirt that looked absolutely ludicrous and useless on him.

If he wasn't sure he'd picked out the hottest oh-hell-no suit he got confirmation quickly. No sooner had he stepped off the bottom step when laughter and a chorus of "oh hell no" rang out. He couldn't stop grinning; he was that *meow* the cat looked for.

Trustee Noel gave a *let's get this party started* nod to Porky. He smiled and watched Porky drag his tired butt over and adjust the dirty chef hat he wore. Then the two strode into the center of the room.

A picture of Ma and Pa Kettle never looked as messed up as those two did. It took a moment for the laughter to die down, but as soon as it did, Trustee Noel spoke. His self-confidence had grown tremendously over the past few weeks and it showed when it shouldn't. The same hand he normally used to twirl that hair sprig he now used to lay on Porky's massive shoulder.

Porky closed his eyes and fell asleep standing up.

"I'm so glad to see y'all," the trustee said. "God is good, the weather is unseasonably warm, ain't too many fools in the place tonight, and we're gonna have a good time."

Glaring at Porky, Freddie Noel grabbed

his golf cap by its lid, pushed it back and to the side, then jabbed one of his skinny fingers into the meaty part of Porky's shoulder to wake him.

The non-too subtle push prompted Porky to wake and scream out, "Yeah, he sho' loves to ball." Trustee Noel paid money for that, too. *I'd a come out cheaper if I'd just hired Little Richard.*

Earlier when the trustee asked Porky if he could imitate Little Richard, Porky claimed he could. The truth was that the closest he ever got to imitating Little Richard was putting one leg on a stool.

Trustee Noel made the rounds, personally shaking hands, giving the ladies pecks on their cheeks, and almost breaking his wrist when he tried to high-five a couple deacons.

Moments later he finally reached where the reverend and Sister Betty stood. No shame in the trustee's game as he feigned a chest bump against his pastor and exclaimed, "You da man!"

Reverend Tom was again speechless. In all his life, he'd never given or received a chest bump before. He quickly looked down at his cross to make sure the Jesus image was okay.

And then to show how much he'd totally changed — or lost — his mind, Trustee

Noel kissed Sister Betty on her lips.

Shocked, she jumped back and fished around inside her pocketbook for her spray can of blessed oil. She didn't know what he'd do next. If he tried to chest bump her, too, she would knee him in the groin.

"My oh my," Trustee Noel smacked his lips as though Sister Betty was a two-piece and a biscuit. "You look beautiful. There ain't nothing like a seasoned-woman of God."

The trustee didn't know what hit him. One minute he stood telling Sister Betty in his own way how good she looked. The next minute Sister Betty and Reverend Tom had hauled his skinny butt back up the stairs to his room.

But before they dragged him away, Reverend Tom said to the shocked guests, "One of y'all bless the food, then please go ahead and eat, drink non-alcoholic drinks, and be merry. We'll be back in a few."

Upstairs in the trustee's room Reverend Tom and Sister Betty questioned his sanity.

"What has happened to you?" Reverend Tom asked the question while he surveyed the room cluttered with new clothes.

"Ain't nothing wrong with me," Trustee Noel replied. He began to feel put upon and they had no right to do that. Didn't he just help them find the Promised Land? "Y'all got no right to drag me off in front of company like that. What did I do wrong?"

The trustee's last question was directed at Sister Betty. Everything he'd done lately was with her in mind. Yet, she'd helped to embarrass him.

Just as the reverend had noticed a huge change in the trustee, Sister Betty did, too. She saw the new clothes and the new television still boxed in a corner. She also noticed the enormous pile of gift-wrapped Mary Kay boxes in another corner. Although neither had exchanged a gift, Christmas was over unless he had a head start on next year's.

It looked as though the trustee had caught a sale from every store in Pelzer. She looked again in the corner and couldn't figure why he'd purchased a great deal of Mary Kay.

While the reverend and the trustee had their heart-to-heart, Sister Betty sat on the only chair in the room. It was hard to imagine that, over the years, she'd never heard the trustee voice an opinion above a whisper, say an unkind word about anyone, or wear anything that didn't smack of a used clothes store. Even when he'd won his millions, for a long time, he'd remained the same. The change, in her opinion, began when he'd tried to rescue his church. Why had that happened?

She stood, and over the music and chatter that filtered its way upstairs, she asked, "Reverend Tom, can I have a few words with Trustee Noel alone please?"

While the reverend and Sister Betty raked the trustee over the coals upstairs, downstairs, the party turned in a new direction. The crowd began celebrating by discussing various ways the Promised Land would improve their lives.

Alice "Grandma Puddin' " Tart stood behind a long table with a string of holly about her sagging neck. A torn hairnet covered her gray wig, but she was overjoyed. While she scooped and tossed mashed potatoes, corn, roast chicken parts, collards, and peas onto their plates, she told the other guests, "Thank the Lord, they got a new medical center in the Promised Land. I can't wait to be able to see a doctor without giving up my mortgage money for a couple pills." She danced a little two-step as she continued to heap generous portions.

"Just having a window to look out and see the highway will be the high point for me." The excitement came from ole man Sheffy. He'd slept under the highway for so many years he almost wept at the thought of seeing it from a distance. He pulled out an envelope from his pants pocket that no longer hung around his knees. "I got my notice today. I got an apartment in the Promised Land."

One by one, the guests shared their hopes and desires of blessings to come for the new year. The few who knew for certain they'd made it into the Promised Land cried and thanked God.

Reverend Tom stepped off the bottom step just in time to hear all the testimonies, hopes, and dreams of those in the community. "This is what it's always been about," he murmured.

Suddenly the unexplained change he'd seen in the trustee diminished for that moment. Only weeks ago people had lost hope in the government, faith in him, and wondered how God fit into the chaos. That night some of those same breathed a sigh of relief and mentally decorated their new homes. Listening to the joy and relief from Alice "Grandma Puddin' " was a blessing in itself.

He waded into the crowd and began to party with them. He didn't even mind when a young man asked him to bless a "sammich" as he called it. "Thank you, Mr. Leotis," the young man said.

That night Reverend Tom didn't mind coming out of the mental pulpit he carried twenty-four-seven. He was going to enjoy those same blessings with the others and on common ground.

CHAPTER 31

Upstairs, inside Trustee Noel's small room everything Sister Betty wanted to say flew out the window. It'd taken off as soon as he went down on one knee. She was never certain of his age, but had figured it was pretty much close to her own. If that were true, then they had a problem. Whatever he got down there to do, she couldn't help him rise when he was finished.

Out of respect, he flipped his golf cap back around to wear it the correct way. He wouldn't look so hip-hop or like a sixty-five-year-old fool.

Sister Betty didn't recall putting her hand on that spray canister of blessed oil. She only knew that the next moment, she had doused him from his golf hat to his ugly black penny loafers.

If she thought a can of prayed-over PAM was going to stop that trustee, then she was as wrong as she'd been about God giving her a break.

"Sister Betty, please." Trustee Noel shoved the canister away from him and tried to pry open the small ring box in his hand. His hand kept slipping off the lid because she'd sprayed him good with that oil. "I just want to ask you something."

She reeled back and let go again, circling him with the spray lever set on BLAST THAT DEMON. "Don't you try and touch me. Watch it now, 'cause I'm touched by God alone."

If she'd been the hot Super Saint mama he thought she was, then he'd have gone up in flames. She wasn't playing about setting his world on fire.

Yet nothing she said deterred Trustee Freddie Noel. He thought he was the Jay-Z of the church. "Jay-Z said it was a hard knock life and Beyoncé says I need to put a ring on it!"

Sister Betty hit him upside his head with the can.

While the trustee and Sister Betty fought over the rules of engagements upstairs, Bea and Sasha finally squared off again, inside Porky's kitchen.

From the time they arrived, most of the guests had placed a bet on how long it

289

would take those two fighting hens to start pecking. Some folks made a lot of money that night and figured out their tithe portion.

The BS fight started as it usually did, with Sasha accusing Bea of stealing. Actually, it was a continuation of their fight from the Seniors Prom. The untimely arrival of Reverend Tom had put a halt to it that night. A simple question reignited the feud.

Alice "Grandma Puddin' " had scooped until her hand hurt, but the guests kept coming back for more. Even Porky ate two helpings despite never getting compliments on anything he cooked. She knew she could put her "foot in a pot." For years, people gave that compliment when she served up a meal.

Sasha had a strong reputation for tossing a meal or two, also, and Bea was the known Queen. But Alice didn't like Bea as much as she liked Sasha, so she directed her attention to Sasha.

When Alice saw Sasha still had food on her plate, she straightened her apron, walked over and asked humbly, "Mother Sasha, cook to cook, how does the food taste?"

And that's when Sasha realized she'd placed her teeth in a cup, but didn't remem-

ber where she set it down. Of course, she
never answered Alice's question. She bowed
her head and slipped into her mouth an
extra pair of teeth she'd brought. But she
wasn't letting it go. She was going to blame
Bea like the last time. She calmly walked
over to where Bea stood, still attached to
Elder Batty Brick.

"Bea," Sasha said sweetly. "May I see you
in the kitchen for a moment?"

CHAPTER 32

It wasn't easy separating Bea and Sasha. It took the combined strength of Reverend Tom, Elder Batty Brick, Brother Casanova, and Porky.

The men had just started to discuss holding another meeting for community outreach at the Soul Food Shanty when they overheard the commotion. In an instant, they dashed into Porky's kitchen and found the old hens pecking.

Before the Christian Cavalry and Porky arrived the old women had managed to bust an angel figure holding a ribbon with JOY TO THE WORLD written upon it. Not too far from the angel lay two holly wreaths that had been one. Even the silver pinecones bound with a beautiful, deep purple sash looked like wood chips. They'd torn that kitchen asunder.

Sasha panted, completely out of breath. She felt strange, so she put her thumb quickly in her mouth and felt nothing but gums. She had lost her spare false teeth as well as ripped the slit in her skirt up another two or three inches. Of course, she'd forgotten to wear drawers again, too.

Bea suffered as well. The men were shocked to see tiny rows of micro gray hairs, making it look like she had a head full of toasted sesame seeds. Her bright mauve-colored wig lay on top of the toaster that had turned on during their fight. The smell of synthetic hair and Royal Crown hair grease was enough to shut down the place. There was a faint odor of urine or some knock-off brand of Summer's Eve feminine deodorizer.

Up in his room Sister Betty didn't need to help Trustee Noel to his feet. He hopped up and was on his way out the door before she said another word. The two of them heard the commotion downstairs and that put an end to the trustee's disastrous marriage proposal.

Instead of following him out of the room, she collapsed onto his bed and looked around his tiny room. Nothing at that moment made sense. Her world was as out of order as his room. In all her visions and knee pains, she'd not seen this one coming.

She questioned her feelings. Did she enjoy the quirky man's company? *Yes.* Had she wanted to become more than friends? *Yes.* She'd like that, but not at that moment and especially not at the Soul Food Shanty. She felt as though he'd taken her to a cliff overlooking a beautiful valley, told her to fly with him or to drop like a rock.

And where was the romance? A woman her age, despite years of being single, still wanted romance. At least, she thought she did. Sister Betty rose and went to the small window in the room. She looked out at the moonlight and the stars, and smiled. "Well, Lord," Sister Betty whispered. "You certainly know how to call the shots."

Just as she turned away from the window, the door opened slightly. With a big grin on her face, Cheyenne walked in the room.

The two old women embraced and Cheyenne apologized for not returning for the ribbon cutting ceremony. "My old rheumatoid held me prisoner again," she explained. "I should've known that as soon as I felt the weather had warmed up a bit and I came back to Pelzer, it would get cold again."

"I know how you feel," Sister Betty said with a smile. "My knee's been revolting for days."

"I see Bea and Sasha got the party started

again." Cheyenne shook her head and switched her cane to the other hand. She pointed to the floor and added, "One day those two old birds gonna figure out just how much they really like one another. When they do this is gonna be one boring town."

Sister Betty didn't agree with Cheyenne's observation. She thought it was absurd. "I've known Bea and Sasha for about as long as I've known you. I've never seen them do anything but bicker, fight, gossip, and gamble."

"That's right," Cheyenne said. She eased down onto the trustee's bed and laid her cane to the side. "And who do they fight with?"

"They fight each other."

"Do you ever see them fight anyone else?"

"Rarely," Sister Betty replied. "They usually reserve a beat down, as the young folks say, for each other."

"And do you think anyone else would put up with their nonsense?"

"No, I don't." Sister Betty suddenly started laughing. It felt good. She'd wanted and needed that laugh. "So, they fight one another because they don't have to worry about the outcome. Come to think of it, I ain't never known either of them to get really hurt or go to a hospital."

"And they never will. Other folks would've nailed their old butts to the wall a long time ago. That's why they always end up at the same place, the same time, and pretend they didn't want to."

Dispensing with thoughts of Bea and Sasha, Sister Betty took a moment and recounted the ribbon cutting ceremony. "Oh, I just thank the Lord." She became excited when she told Cheyenne who'd attended.

"Oh, and I thank the Lord," she repeated after she gave an account on how the reverend made his confession before the congregation. "He didn't hold back. The reverend admitted how he'd distanced himself from the members and thought he was so much better."

Cheyenne interrupted with a question. She hadn't become as excited as Sister Betty appeared to be. "Did he tell them that his grandmother was a whore?"

"Yes, he did. He not only talked about how her money had blessed him and the church, then he accepted how others' monies had done the same."

"Good for him," Cheyenne said and winked. "There's hope there after all."

Once that conversation was exhausted,

Cheyenne began to laugh and look about the room.

"What's so funny?" Sister Betty looked around the room, too.

"Just wondering when you are going to give Trustee Noel his answer and take him out of this dump. He doesn't seem to want to leave on his own, even though he can buy the whole block."

"What are you talking about?" Sister Betty hadn't mentioned one word about what had happened earlier. She was certain Cheyenne hadn't time to talk to the trustee. Why would she?

"Honey, I helped him pick out the ring when he took me out to lunch the other day." Cheyenne squirmed on the bed to get comfortable.

"The other day, what are you talking about?"

Cheyenne explained that she'd felt bad about how she treated him at the Seniors Prom and reached out to apologize. During their conversation, he asked questions about Sister Betty and confessed his growing feelings.

"He said you and he 'fit like a hand in a glove'," Cheyenne quoted. "I told him not to lay a glove on you, but do like Beyoncé said, and lay a ring on you instead."

297

"You had no right to tell him that." Sister Betty became annoyed, but only a little bit.

"Oh Betty, please," Cheyenne rebuked. "It ain't like the two of you got from now on to get it together."

"That's not the point," Sister Betty replied. "We're not in love."

"Have you ever been in love besides being in love with Jesus?"

Sister Betty didn't quite know how to respond. The only time in her life she could recall having such feelings was when she was a teenager. At seventeen, she'd given up her virginity in her parents' barn, become pregnant, then lost the baby months later. She'd not been close to feeling like that since.

Sister Betty hadn't meant for Cheyenne to see the pain on her face, although she was certain she had. "I guess I don't know what love is."

"Honey, look," Cheyenne said as she moved over so Sister Betty could sit closer. "The time for all those pie in the sky, moonlight kisses, and star spangled banner playing are over for you and Freddie. Y'all are too close to crossing over to waste a lot of time on regrets. I'm not telling you that you have to marry him next week, but if you feel anything close to what his feelings are, then be honest and give it a chance. I can tell you one thing . . ."

"What's that?" Sister Betty asked, although not sure if she wanted to know.

"This particular Christmas season and that particular Freddie Noel ain't no ordinary Noels."

Trustee Noel barged into the room with that golf cap folded and crammed in his hand with a wild look upon his face. It meant one thing. Something had gone wrong, very wrong.

"I'm sorry, Sister Betty, but I need Miss Cheyenne right away." He started rocking side-to-side and was about to yank that sprig of hair completely off his scalp.

Cheyenne reached for her cane. "What's wrong with you?"

"Has something happened downstairs?" Sister Betty asked. She fought hard against showing any jealousy since he'd asked for Cheyenne and not her.

"I'm sorry Sister Betty. You ain't fit for this type of mess and dousing folks won't work. I need Miss Cheyenne's help."

Cheyenne finally inched her way off the bed, checked her hair to make sure it was still pinned, and slowly made it to Trustee Noel's side. "What is wrong with you? Is it Bea and Sasha?"

"No ma'am. It's much worse," the trustee's yellow complexion looked jaundiced.

"What can be worse than Bea and Sasha?" Sister Betty couldn't imagine anything worse than the trouble they made.

"Again, I apologize to you, Sister Betty." He was so frantic he almost lifted Cheyenne off the floor. Without stopping to see if she was ready to leave the room, he pointed at the boxes in the corner and told Sister Betty, "Why don't you just help yourself to any of those Mary Kay gifts. We'll be back shortly."

And that's when Cheyenne looked at the stack of gift-wrapped Mary Kay boxes and fell out laughing. She turned and faced poor Freddie and asked, "Did you get all those boxes from where I think you got 'em?"

"Yes, ma'am, I did."

"Oh my goodness," Cheyenne replied as she led him out of the room. "It was your first time, wasn't it?"

"Yes, ma'am, it was." Freddie glanced back at Sister Betty and whispered, "I'm so sorry."

CHAPTER 33

During the time Cheyenne and Sister Betty were upstairs, people came and went inside the Soul Food Shanty. Many stopped by because they'd heard about the private celebration and wanted to be included. If the media came by, they wanted to be there.

However, one had more on her mind than a mere television appearance. She watched for most of the evening with her eyes glued on the reverend and the trustee. She waited until most of the accolades were given and cell phone camera shots were taken of the two men before she made a move.

The two men had separate appeal; one had the looks, the position, the style, and the youth. The other had nothing more than a million bucks. She struggled to choose.

Thirty-five-year-old former Mary Kay Cosmetic Consultant Shaniqua Burke walked slowly toward the take-out counter near the door to the Shanty. Shaniqua, a mulatto former beauty queen from New Orleans, attended the At Last Disciple Temple in Belton. She was a size six vixen in a red curly wig that framed her oval face and accented her big brown eyes. The false hair cascaded past her shoulders and stopped at breasts so big they blocked her hair from falling any farther.

Shaniqua slowly pulled a stool away from the counter and laid her purse upon it. Then, as Nat King Cole's "chestnuts roasting on an open fire" flowed from squeaky speakers, she slowly removed her fur wrap, and showed her true skills. She also showed her toned thighs and bared her snow-white teeth. Men and flies fell out around the Shanty, and she'd not even begun to speak.

Her silent sermon was so good that even a few of the female doubters became converted.

Shaniqua pretended not to notice that all eyes were upon her and she dropped a napkin from the counter. She bent over. If she ever decided to preach, she showed from where she'd take her text. When she stood again, Cheyenne had joined her.

"Shaniqua," Cheyenne said loudly. "Cut it out."

"I'm just trying to sell —"

Cheyenne cut her off. "I know what you're

trying to sell. I see boxes of it upstairs."

Meanwhile the reverend wasn't immune to a soul in need of saving, so he walked over and made his introduction.

Cheyenne stood to the side to watch Lillie's grandbaby in action.

"Oh, I know who you are," Shaniqua purred. "You're that pastor who was crazy enough to turn down more than a million dollars." She stopped and placed her hand on one hip. "I must say that you look like a million, so maybe that's why you turned it down. I'd sure hate to think you were stupid."

Upon hearing the word *stupid,* the trustee got enough nerve and walked over to stand next to Cheyenne.

"How are you doing, Miss Shaniqua?" Freddie asked with perspiration pricking his skin. "I really don't need any more products. I haven't used what I bought from you."

No one saw Bea, Alice "Grandma Puddin'," and Sasha rush toward the Shanty door. Bea almost knocked Cheyenne over as she swooped up the purse and Shaniqua with it. Alice "Grandma Puddin' " held the Shanty's door open, and Sasha used her cane to convince Shaniqua to leave.

"Don't nobody take out the trash no more?" Sasha hissed as she kicked Shaniqua's fur out the door behind her.

"We got yo' back Cheyenne," Alice "Grandma Puddin' " snapped. "That heffa-fied niece of yours won't be back to bother nobody."

"I didn't need help with Shaniqua," Cheyenne barked. "This was family business. I could've dealt with it."

"But ya didn't and we did," Bea replied angrily.

Bea didn't wait for a reply from Cheyenne. She turned away and received a high-five from Sasha. "Come on Smurf," Bea said as she led Sasha away, "we won't stop lookin' until we find yo teeth. That Shaniqua's one problem we hafta keep on solving. Ya think that little hussy would leave Pelzer boys alone."

It took the reverend a moment to realize he needed to thank his busybody church mothers. He'd relaxed his guard a little too much and almost stepped into more drama. He could see his reputation sullied and the loss of confidence in the Promised Land if he'd proceeded to a place where lust had almost led him.

Cheyenne quickly got over her disappoint-ment in how her niece always acted and chatted with the trustee for a moment.

Trustee Noel apologized to Cheyenne if

304

he led Shaniqua on when he'd bought up her Mary Kay supplies. "I was only trying to help her make that quota she kept complaining about. She was your niece so I didn't think anything more about it until she showed up here tonight asking for me. Brother Casanova told me what she really wanted and it wasn't something I wanna give away all willy-nilly."

Cheyenne stepped back and looked at the trustee. She sized him up and down and then smiled. "You mean you ain't never given it up willy-nilly or otherwise?"

His complexion turned beet-red, and he fidgeted with the cap he still held. He wouldn't answer her question directly, but said, "I think I might've misread Sister Betty. It didn't go too well upstairs."

Cheyenne smiled and patted him on the shoulder. "I believe you need to go back upstairs and reread that book."

CHAPTER 34

Standing with a cup of coffee in his hand, Reverend Tom squinted his eyes as he repeatedly looked out his window for any sign of Sister Betty.

The celebration at the Soul Food Shanty had lasted well past midnight, although many people left earlier because they had to work the next morning. Elder Batty Brick took Bea away, hopefully back to her house. Brother Casanova complained, but finally gave in, and after shutting off his hearing aid, he'd taken Sasha away. Fortunately, Alice "Grandma Puddin' " had driven her Ford Focus. Once all the pots and pans were secured, there was enough room for Cheyenne in the Ford Focus, so she took Cheyenne back to spend the night at her house.

Reverend Tom had driven home alone once Trustee Noel insisted and promised that he had a way of getting Sister Betty back home at a reasonable hour.

The reverend turned and rekindled the fire in his fireplace. Before he returned to look out the window to see if she'd returned yet, he called her home again. And again, her answering machine picked up. He didn't bother to leave a message seeing as how it would be no different from the other that he'd left. He could only imagine how a father felt about his children. At that moment, he worried about Sister Betty as though she were a small child.

Trustee Noel, no longer in his oil-soaked casual suit, fingered the ring box in his pocket. The limousine he'd reserved to take Sister Betty back to her home still idled at a vacant spot on the Promised Land. They'd stopped there to see it in the moonlight and now it was almost sunup.

The two had come together back at the Shanty and talked. They'd dispensed with the notion of puppy love and put their cards on the table. Sister Betty finally decided she'd accept his friendship, but not the ring. It was a bit too much, and too soon.

The trustee heard Sister Betty say "not now." In his mind, that didn't mean the same thing as "not ever." He decided to keep the ring in his pocket no matter what

307

he wore and if the time came when they both felt the same he'd give it to her then.

"Can you imagine how Mother Ide De-Clare will feel when she no longer has to stay on the ground floor because she's in a wheelchair and the elevator doesn't work?" Sister Betty asked. "I can almost taste the freedom it will bring her."

"She, Alice 'Grandma Puddin' ' and many of the poor will be a lot better off once they've moved into the Promised Land." Trustee Noel let a smile creep across his face. He suddenly started to giggle like a little kid. "You'll never guess what I've done."

Sister Betty couldn't imagine and wasn't sure if she wanted to know. However, his silly laugh caused her to laugh, too, but only he knew why. "What did you do now?"

"I got a hold of the apartment plans for the seniors building."

"That's not bad. You would've gotten it sooner or later since you're on the Selecting Committee."

"I know," Trustee Noel said as his laughter grew. He only brought down the volume when the driver looked back, apparently thinking something was wrong. "You can't tell anyone."

"I won't. What did you do?"

Trustee Noel leaned over and conspired. "I finagled with the selections and put Bea and Sasha in apartments next to each other." Trustee Noel leaned back and slapped his bony knee. He had tears running down his face from laughing so hard.

Sister Betty was worse. She grabbed a box of tissues, used them all, and still couldn't stop the laughing tears.

"Oh my goodness," Sister Betty said through bouts of laughter. "Those two are gonna kill each other."

"I know," Trustee Noel replied. "Won't that be a hoot!"

All during the week, the reverend fussed at Sister Betty. When he wasn't fussing about her coming home so late he fussed that she didn't spend time with him like a good spiritual mom should.

His church became vital and he made a promise at the New Year's Eve Watch Night service that he would show his members and community how much God had reshaped the vessel.

CHAPTER 35

Reverend Tom spent a lot of time visiting the sick and the elderly. He'd always read his Bible, but once Bible study resumed in the new year, unlike in the past when he relied on a deacon or associate minister to teach, he took the responsibility. Every lesson he taught, he learned something, too.

Out of everything that gave him pleasure, and there was a lot that did, the blessing of overseeing the Promised Land topped the list. It seemed the more he grew in God the less problematic the construction.

The only ones that made complaints were the Cheater Brothers. They hadn't enticed any of the members or Trustee Noel to return their savings to the Piece of Savings Bank. The Cheaters weren't happy with the millions they made off the Promised Land. As far as the reverend was concerned, they needed to take that up with God, and he didn't mean their Wall Street idol.

Over the course of several months the Promised Land became more structured and businesses vied for an opportunity to open or expand in the facilities. The demand on the reverend's time and input increased. Except for a dinner every now and again, church services, and a glance from their porches, he and Sister Betty were like ships passing in the night.

Trustee Noel relaxed a little in pursuing Sister Betty as his love interest and enjoyed her friendship. It took him a while to convince her that moving out of the Soul Food Shanty apartment and into a huge house around the corner from her didn't mean he was a stalker.

He paid Porky a year's advance rent on his old room before he moved out. Porky was fine with the deal until he discovered the trustee had subleased the room. Ole Sheffy, the wino, wouldn't have to wait until the senior housing was complete before he had a roof over his head that didn't have cars running on it.

Trustee Noel promised God that he'd make a difference with the lottery money. He wasn't satisfied with tithing and bailing out the church for the Promised Land. He wanted more for Pelzer. He became very interested in how he could make life better for the youth, and brought in young successful business people to talk to the youth about their entrepreneurial possibilities.

However, of all the new and improved ventures Trustee Noel financed over the past year, there was one of which he was the most proud. Despite many naysayers, he expanded the church's prison ministry. It took months, but many men and women, although physically incarcerated, finally accepted God's grace, mercy, and forgiveness. They learned they were not spiritually locked away from Jesus. Furthermore, almost ninety percent of these men and women used their time well. Some went on to receive high school diplomas, and others proudly accepted long-awaited college degrees. They'd become Trustee Noel's seeds, planted for a fruitful harvest upon their release.

CHAPTER 36

Promised Land Open for Business

"You know you're wrong for that Freddie," Sister Betty had warned the trustee several months ago. He'd laughed it off again. She'd had a chance to think it over and believed that what he'd done would upset the balance of peace. But Trustee Noel didn't listen and refused to separate Bea and Sasha's names on the list to be neighbors.

When the Promised Land opened three months later, Bea and Sasha ended up next-door neighbors on the second floor in one of the senior citizen residential buildings. Their bedrooms were so close they could hear each other snore. Yet, as much as they claimed to dislike each other they had keys to each other's apartment. "It's just in case . . . ," they said.

Because of the trustee's prank, the building named LILLIAN SINCLAIR, after the

Reverend's famous grandmother, became more notorious than its namesake.

It hardly seemed possible that it was Christmastime again. The Promised Land had become a mecca in Pelzer. Everyone found a way there for one reason or another.

Christmas Eve brought particular joy and it showed. Earlier that evening the Christmas Pageant was held inside the new recreation center on the Promised Land. It went without a hitch. Normally the business side of the Promised Land along with the Health Care Center stayed open and busy until nine o'clock at night, but all the buildings decorated with their colorful lights and animated figures drew crowds late into the night. The cash registers inside the stores overflowed with money and store clerks raced to restock and keep up.

Although it was dark, and the children were supposed to be home awaiting a visit from Santa, they gathered with the seniors and watched beautiful red, white, blue, yellow, and green lights flash MERRY CHRISTMAS from the Promised Land. It was a miracle. Cars hurried along Highway 29, no doubt to reach their destination before midnight. Yet they slowed down and some even honked their horns to show appreciation for the Promised Land lighted welcome.

As peaceful as it was outside with Christmas carols provided by the youth choir singing a cappella, there was enough drama unfolding on the second floor of the Lillie Sinclair building to make it seem more like Halloween than Christmas Eve.

After the pageant, Bea bounced around her living room as if she'd been stung by a wasp. She whooped, bucked, and almost collapsed before jumping up and starting all over again. "Oh Jesus," she screamed. "Oh Lord!" She alternated between grabbing hold of the strap of her white angel costume that fell off one shoulder, and trying to pull the cinnamon-streaked wig back onto her head. Every time she hopped around each threatened to fall off.

Next door, Sasha stood inside her shower stall. She hummed and danced a little side-to-side move, while lathered from neck to feet with her favorite body foam, Purple Delusion. She stopped everything when she heard a noise from Bea's apartment.

Sasha didn't bother to rinse. She hopped out of the shower, hurried and put her ear to the wall. The noise sounded like moans, but she couldn't tell if Bea was having heart attack or if someone was attacking her.

Either way, Sasha didn't want to miss it.

She threw a beach towel around her lathered nakedness, grabbed the key to Bea's apartment, and raced next door.

She didn't knock or ring Bea's doorbell. She jammed the key in the door and dashed inside, stopping short as soon as she saw Elder Batty Brick, dressed as Santa with a bow tied about his neck. He was kneeling on one knee while Bea stood over the man, jumping up and down, screaming like a banshee. She kept turning her ring finger side to side. Bea wore a diamond that dazzled on her finger.

Neither Bea nor Elder Batty Brick heard Sasha when she first entered, but they certainly learned quickly that she was there.

When Sasha saw the ring on Bea's finger, she hollered, "You got a ring!" Then she pointed at Elder Santa Claus Batty Brick, still on one knee and she screamed again, "You gave that She-Rilla a ring!"

It was enough to make Sasha drop her towel and with her body still covered with foam she looked like a miniature Mrs. Frosty, except with legs shaped like parentheses.

It was more than enough to make Bea scream again. Sasha screamed even more and Elder Batty Brick simply tossed his

Santa hat aside and reached for his glasses.

In Bea's one second of clarity, she thought either Sasha didn't realize she'd dropped her towel or she'd tried to tempt Bea's new fiancé. Either way, Bea saw it for its worst and almost crushed Elder Batty Brick as she stepped on his glasses on her way to kill Sasha.

Sasha and Bea circled and tormented one another with accusations and faked punches. They would've hit each other for real, but Bea didn't want to mess up the ring. She hadn't had it appraised yet. And Sasha tried to save her foam and her assets.

While Bea and Sasha pecked away in Bea's apartment, Brother Casanova stepped off the elevator onto the second floor. He'd become accustomed to turning his hearing aid volume down or off whenever he was around Sasha, so he heard nothing unusual.

Earlier that evening, Sasha had sent word she needed to see Brother Casanova and that she had a special gift. He didn't have anything to do and after all, it was Christmas Eve. He didn't want to be alone, and who didn't like gifts?

Brother Casanova had to pass by Bea's apartment on his way to Sasha's. If the door to Bea's apartment wasn't open, if Sasha hadn't squirmed trying to avoid Bea's grasp and now looked like a rabid bat with a bun on her head, and if Elder Batty Brick wasn't dressed like Santa, he might've kept walking.

A stunned Brother Casanova tripped over Bea's WELCOME mat and piled into the room. Sasha had just rewrapped the towel about her embarrassment, but he ripped it away when he fell.

Then they all went to kung fu fighting.

Sister Betty, Trustee Noel, and Reverend Tom visited the first floor apartment of Alice "Grandma Puddin'." She'd invited them for a Christmas Eve repast along with Cheyenne Bigelow. Unfortunately, Alice's apartment was directly below Bea's apartment.

Reverend Tom had just spoken the word AMEN after blessing the food when paint chips from the ceiling fell into the bowl of mashed yams. Alice was certain she hadn't added any marshmallows, but at her age, she wasn't too certain. It wasn't the first time there'd been noises coming from Bea's apartment. There wasn't peace and quiet on any given night since she'd started regularly dating Elder Batty Brick. Everyone ignored the hollering and sounds of furniture moving about.

However, when Alice's chandelier started swinging and a few pictures fell off the walls, it became a concern. No one wanted to get involved in whatever was happening in Bea's apartment, but since they blamed Trustee Noel for being such a busybody in the first place, they insisted he go upstairs and see about it. The rest stayed behind and praised Alice for the new ingredient in the mashed yams.

CHAPTER 37

He hadn't been inside but about ten minutes, before Trustee Noel stood beside Bea's couch with his head in his hands. They worried him so much he twirled that sprig down to one hair, and he was protecting it at all cost.

From the moment he'd walked into Bea's apartment, everyone had given him an excuse for the drama. It took him a few minutes to adjust his eyes after seeing Sasha in a state he never wanted to see again. Although, he thought that had he been a lot younger, he might've appreciated those parentheses-shaped legs of hers.

He took Elder Batty Brick and Brother Casanova to the side to discuss what to do about "their" women. Of course, the men reminded him that he caused it in the first place when he put them side by side. And that's when Trustee Noel reminded the men that Bea and Sasha had lived across town from one another for decades, and always found a way to peck at each other.

While the men stood over in a corner assessing and passing blame, Bea and Sasha stood in the kitchen. Bea had her refrigerator door open with its bright light shining on her ring finger. Sasha also held a flashlight on the ring just in case they missed something with the refrigerator light.

"It's gorgeous, Bea. And I'm sorry I made such a mess of your engagement. I thought you were hurt." Sasha had mixed a lie somewhere in the truth. She smiled, forgetting she didn't have her false teeth in, as she turned Bea's ring finger back and forth under the flashlight. "It looks like your cooking done finally paid off."

"Well, thank you Sasha," Bea replied, "but ya know when I put it in an oven, it will bake." She couldn't help but laugh at her own pun.

Any other time Bea would've challenged Sasha's lie instead of laughing with her, but not tonight. She'd spoiled Elder Batty Brick beyond rotten and her red velvet cake sealed the deal. Besides, seeing Sasha bald in the mouth and everywhere it counted made Bea feel sorry for her. She forgave Sasha and loaned her one of her robes.

Bea and Sasha rejoined the men in the

living room. Of course, Bea immediately flew to Elder Batty Brick's side and showed the ring to Trustee Noel. She apologized for the disruption and gave Sasha a hug to prove all was well.

"So when is the big day?" Trustee Noel asked. He really wanted to know when and if Elder Batty Brick would move Bea out so peace could return to the Lillie Sinclair.

"I just proposed tonight," Elder Batty Brick replied. "Bea ain't even said yes yet."

Everyone in the room looked at Elder Batty Brick with his Santa Hat torn into strips as though he'd lost his mind.

Bea and Sasha started laughing. They laughed so hard they had to lean on one another to stand up. Finally, Bea was able to speak coherently. "Well, suh," she started as she looked at her new fiancé. "In the kitchen me and my best friend talked about my deep love and appreciation for ya. She shined a light on something and I'm con- vinced that I wanna be a Brick."

Elder Batty Brick couldn't get the grin off his face, but it didn't stop his mouth from asking a stupid question. "That's wonderful Bea" — he looked around — "but when am I gonna meet your best friend who showed you the light?"

That's when Sasha clocked him in the

chest with the flashlight and started singing, "This little light of mine."

Later on that night, after Sister Betty had said her good-byes to Cheyenne, Alice "Grandma Puddin'," and Reverend Tom, she climbed into the limousine and moved closer to the trustee.

They didn't speak for a while, preferring to watch the beautiful and colorful Christmas lights fade into the shadows of the Promised Land.

The surroundings were beautiful and the ride peaceful, but the trustee's thoughts went in all directions. Before the fiasco at Bea's apartment, he had Christmas Eve all planned and Sister Betty would've loved it. He could've beaten last year's pig feet out of Elder Batty Brick, but then he had himself to blame.

He should never have told the elder that he planned to propose to Sister Betty again. Elder Brick had upped him one and proposed to Bea first. It wouldn't have been too much of a problem had not Bea and Sasha been Bea and Sasha and disrupted Christmas Eve. He wouldn't be surprised to learn that Santa took another route and bypassed the Promised Land's children all together.

To get more comfortable Sister Betty opened her white lamb's wool coat at the neck. The trustee had it handmade for her as a Christmas present. She'd given him a thousand dollar gift certificate to Jos. A. Bank just to get him away from JCPenney.

She removed the matching hat without disturbing her wig. She sighed and laid her head back against the softness of the limo's heated leather seat. She took another peek at the beautiful scenery that flashed as they rode. Without saying a word, she smiled, hugged her Bible to her chest, closed her eyes, and daydreamed on how God had begun to deal with her in a different way.

My knees don't ache quite as much. I've seen Cheyenne travel from Belton to Pelzer for services at least twice each month and for an elderly white woman with rheumatoid arthritis, she outshouts most.

I've prayed and fasted on a particular matter, and called on God to show me how His need for me would affect a married life, mine in particular, if it were to happen. I've never been married nor been asked so have never brought it before the Throne.

Why have I become so comfortable with a man I've known for years without really getting to know him during that time? I enjoy his

324

visits, don't find him as unattractive as some, love the way he twirls his sprig of hair. I appreciate his ironic wit and the constant shower of approval and praises he heaps without provocation. Most of all, I love the way the trustee loves the Lord.

I've never lived with anyone before and yet he fits so comfortably at my kitchen table when we dine at my home.

Forgetting for the moment that she daydreamed, she murmured, "Lord, what could possibly be wrong with this man?"

And then God, with his eternal sense of humor, pulled back the cover of Sister Betty's eyes and ears.

The trustee snored. He sounded like an old-time train engine choking on his own smoke.

The ball was now in her corner.

Before they knew it, the limo pulled into Sister Betty's driveway. Trustee Noel got out and walked her to her door, being careful that she didn't slip on the path.

They laughed when they saw the light a few doors away, inside Reverend Tom's living room, go out. That meant he'd arrived home before them and had waited up until she got home.

"I see your spiritual son still spies on you,"

the trustee teased. "I guess he thinks I'm a regular Mack Daddy or something."

"Oh he thinks you're something," Sister Betty whispered, and added, "Me, too."

The next morning, Reverend Tom woke to the sound of someone leaning on his doorbell. He grabbed a robe, threw it on, and almost tripped over a hassock as he raced through the living room.

Elder Batty Brick, Brother Casanova, and Trustee Noel stood huddled and shivering with the wind whipping at their backs. No one said a word as each watched the pastor's face contort. They'd each rung the doorbell for no good reason other than they were cold and nervous.

Despite the fact it was Christmas Day, it was almost ten o'clock. The men thought the pastor, a bachelor, too, would be up already.

Reverend Tom told the men where to hang their coats and such while he retreated to the kitchen to make coffee.

"I once looked buff like that," Brother Casanova lied, pointing to the reverend's sculptured physique.

"Youth sure is wasted sometimes," Elder Batty Brick's jealousy showed and he wasn't trying to hide it. "I gotta get my strength back. Man can't live off red velvet cake alone."

"Well I ain't never looked like that and doubt if I ever will." Trustee Noel was the only one who spoke the truth.

Once they sat at the kitchen table, the reverend, still in his pajamas and robe, poured cups of coffee. "What in the world made y'all drop by unexpected on Christmas Day?"

"Bea don't wanna wait to get married," Elder Batty Brick complained as he gulped down the hot liquid.

"And all Betty does is tell me to wait," Trustee Noel said. "I've waited long enough."

The reverend put his cup down and was about to set the trustee straight about Sister Betty, but figured he'd get Brother Casanova's problem on the table first.

"So Brother Casanova," Reverend Tom said. "What's your problem?"

"Oh, I ain't got no women problems," Brother Casanova replied.

"Then why are you here?" The reverend didn't try to hold back his annoyance. "It's Christmas Day," he reminded. "Surely, you had something to do."

"I ain't got nothing to do so I drove 'em here." Brother Casanova took a sip of coffee

327

and added, "Besides, Sasha and them other hens are getting together later on. They done sniffed the air for matrimony and figure it's time to see you married off."

Elder Batty Brick, Trustee Noel, and Brother Casanova were shocked. They'd never seen a grown, muscle-bound, handsome preacher's eyes tear up.

EPILOGUE

Before Moses started on his journey to fulfill God's will, he'd floated in a woven basket as a baby. When he became a young adult, he lived the privileged life in Pharaoh's house. After he'd made Pharaoh angry and discovered he'd been born a slave, Moses' life changed forever.

He went from turning a stick into a snake to leading God's people through the Red Sea with an angry Pharaoh nipping at his heels. Moses' hair turned snow white after trying to lead those same hardheaded, bitter folks who weren't too crazy about eating manna wafers every day.

But Moses wanted to give it all up when he returned from a mountain visitation with God. Confronted with proof that the people had truly lost their minds he became angry to see that they'd melted their gold and other fine metals together and made a very expensive image of a bull to worship.

Reverend Tom finished rereading his sermon notes, made an adjustment here and there as led by the Holy Spirit, then laid his pen down upon the pad. It would be the fourth time he preached from the book of Exodus. Each time, he gained a new appreciation for what Moses had done. The reverend ran his fingers through his hair and along the sides of his scalp. Like Moses, during the past year, he'd sprouted a few white strands as well.

He'd also added a few new items to the wall of his den. They fit well between all the certificates and awards he'd received during the past almost ten years. THE LILLIE SINCLAIR SENIOR CITIZEN CENTER one of the plaques read. IN MEMORY OF LILLIE SINCLAIR was another one.

They were duplicates of the plaque placed on the senior building erected on the Promised Land as well as one placed on the back of the Mothers Board pew. Placing the one on the back of the pew was Bea's idea.

There was also a large picture of his grandmother. She was a striking woman with a cinnamon complexion, huge eyes, and an extremely thin waist. Dressed in the latest fashion of her day with dark hair polished and wavy, she stood alongside several well-known men and women. Their smiles were wide and approving.

He'd come to judge Lillie Sinclair less each time he looked at her picture. He was still human and subject to judgmental tendencies, but God was still working on him.

With the completion and success of the Promised Land, other visions plagued him. There was much work left to do. However, he'd learned to take a step back and wait on God to work His plan, and not plow forward with one of his own.

His eyes had grown a little tired, so he pushed away the pad and placed a marker in the Bible. Rising from the swivel chair in his den, he looked toward Sister Betty's house. "Lord, please help me." He smiled. There were adjustments coming his way and despite his reservations, he'd accepted they would happen.

One of the strangest changes was that Elder Batty Brick and Bea had called off their wedding plans. He'd gotten the call after they'd had it out after Bible study following New Year's Eve.

It appeared that Bea had gotten buyer's remorse when the elder testified that God told him, once he married Bea, to insist she give up playing bingo and hanging out with Sasha. And God didn't want her anywhere near Cheyenne Bigelow. He then told the church that he wanted Bea more domesticated, and if it were possible, barefoot and pregnant.

Bea's response had been, "God knows my number and if He'd wanted such a thing He'd call me, too!" She then kicked him in his butt as he knelt at the altar.

Bea refused to give him back the ring and went on about her business. Strangely, neither seemed to mind the sudden change in the nuptial plans, and the last he'd heard, Elder Batty Brick still went to Bea's for dinner every Sunday after service.

Once Bea had more time to peck with Sasha, then Sasha left Brother Casanova alone. But instead of him leaving well enough alone, he started buying Mary Kay from Cheyenne's scandalous niece, Shaniqua Burke. Reverend Tom could accept all of that except the upcoming change that caused him angst. He picked the invitation off his desk and reread it.

Betty Sarah Becton
&
Freddie Noel
Invite you to share in their joy

as they exchange marriage vows
on Saturday, the Eighteenth of
February
at Seven O'clock in the Evening
Lillie Sinclair Senior Citizen Center
106 East Caroline Street
Pelzer, South Carolina

Reverend Tom laid the announcement on his desk and sat back behind his desk. He opened the pad and reread his sermon notes.

Bea started her dinner cooking around three o'clock the Friday after calling off her wedding. She had just sat to rest when she heard someone pound on her door.

Judging from where the pounding was the loudest, midway in the door, she knew it was Sasha. "What do that little Smurf want now?" Bea slowly opened the door prepared with an excuse not to let her inside, but Sasha was hopping around as though she had to use the bathroom.

Bea's disappointment raced to her face, but she didn't say a word. She turned and went back to her kitchen where she could stir her pots.

All the while, Sasha's mouth was set to

speed chatter and no one could bring it to a halt.

"I can't believe it!" Sasha said. She kept saying it until Bea could take it no longer.

"What is it ya can't believe now?"

"That man is almost broke! He's done give away practically all his money." Sasha pounded Bea's table, causing Bea's cake in the oven to drop.

"What man? Who told ya that?"

"I was downstairs gossip—" Sasha corrected herself. "I was downstairs chatting with Alice 'Grandma Puddin' ' when Cheyenne stopped by 'cause you know she done moved from Belton and now she's living in building three."

"Go on with it, Smurf!"

Sasha pretended she didn't hear Bea's insult because her news was more important at that moment. It didn't mean she wouldn't remember later.

"He done went and spent money on fixing up some of the buildings around Porky's. I also heard Freddie Noel might want to buy a partnership in the Shanty."

Bea was mad, and she threw the spoon she held into the sink. "That fool should've made me part owner. I'd fixed that slop hole up and made a real restaurant out of it."

"Shuddup and let me finish," Sasha

barked. She plopped down onto a chair. "Just thinking about that ignorant man done made me tired."

"You telling it or what?"

"He also gave some more money to the church and they are about to rename the fellowship hall after him. Now I guess he's gonna hafta live off Sister Betty's money unless that insurance settlement ever comes through. Doggone idiot!"

"Don't lump no po' dog in the same mess as that fool," Bea snapped. "I wonder what Sister Betty gonna do about that wedding now. It's gonna take a lot to have it at the Senior Center."

"I don't know what she gone do. But I ain't tol' you the best part yet!"

"Ya means there's more?"

"Yes, ma'am." Sasha pointed to one of Bea's chairs for her to sit in. "Honey, listen. Trustee Soon-To-Be-Broke also got a letter from the IRS."

The women gossiped on, far past the time Bea should've taken out the roast and mashed the potatoes. But Bea and Sasha couldn't believe the irony. The kindhearted, but still foolish, trustee had given away such a huge chunk of his money, he'd received a notice from the IRS in appreciation.

"Oh yeah, one other thing," Sasha said

between bouts of giggles. "He probably never should've bought that house around the corner from Sister Betty."

"Oh stop it, Sasha." Bea grabbed her stomach and hoped her Depend held up. She laughed so hard she began barking. "Have mercy, he should've known better. How was he supposed to go from the Shanty to the most expensive part of town without notice, especially since everybody knows he don't work? Social Security hardly kept him at the Shanty."

Bea pushed away from the table still laughing. She touched the center of the red velvet cake and when it didn't spring back because it'd fallen, she cut a slice from that section and gave it to Sasha.

"Bea, I don't know about you," Sasha confessed as she crammed the cake into her mouth, "but Freddie Noel just ain't ready for primetime. Whatever happened to doing it as the Bible says and giving in a secret closet?"

She stopped chewing and added, "You got anything to drink? This cake is dry."

Bea poured some water into a drinking glass and slammed it down in front of her. She made sure only a little spilled onto her annoying friend before she started talking. "He can forget about a secret closet. It ain't a secret now." Bea handed Sasha a napkin already wet and unusable. "From what ya saying, Uncle Sam bringing his own hangers and peeking in that closet."

Bea stopped laughing and turned serious for a moment. "I'm glad I decided not to get married to Batty Brick and just stay broke with no chance of becoming a millionaire. I don't need another visit through the IRS system, 'cause I ain't been to an IRS family get-together since '83. Just about all my relatives had to make deals or go to the slammer."

"I know what you mean," Sasha whispered. "I'm gonna stay just as blessed with poverty as I can. I don't need no financial microscope on me unless it's part of a biology exam."

Sasha got up and went to the door, with Bea following behind her. She turned and said, "I still don't see how such an ordinary man like Trustee Freddie Noel turned our church and community upside down."

"From what I've heard Cheyenne say, he ain't no ordinary Noel."

"You're right Bea," Sasha took her cane from beside the door where she'd laid it. "I betcha he does something stupid at that wedding. Are you going?"

"I wouldn't miss it. I'm just waiting on an

invite," Bea admitted, then asked, "Did you get one?"

"Of course. I got mine weeks ago." Sasha lied. "You telling me that you didn't get one yet?"

"No, not yet, but I'm sure I will. The three of us been friends all these years, I can't believe Sister Betty would wanna get married and not have me and you there."

Oh, they could believe it. They just didn't *want* to believe it. After all of Bea's and Sasha's years of living and praising their God on Fantasy Island, they refused to accept that not everyone wanted, in their limited thinking, BS on their special day.

'Twas the night before Christmas
And Pookie awoke,
He ran to his piggybank,
Discovered he was broke.

"It's a shame, I'm so po',"
He cried out loud.
Pookie was brave, but
Still broke and still proud.

Broke, but wanting to decorate,
Ran to his closet, open the door.
A box of junk fell out.
Knocked Pookie to the floor.

Out spilled an Easter bunny
Used over a dozen times,
A box of cherry bombs
From July 4th and left behind.

Kicked the boxes aside
And got down on his knees.
"I know I got a baby Jesus —"
But where it was, he couldn't see.

He found a pumpkin from Halloween,
Two black Barbies and a Ken doll.
Wrapped them in some tissue
Carefully, so they wouldn't fall.

Why he had two dolls
Was anybody's guess.
He was determined to have Christmas,
Pookie wanted to be blessed.

He found a shoebox
And filled it with rye bread.
Had no sheep or cows for the manger.
Used that Easter bunny instead.

Pookie grabbed the two Barbies
And the Ken.
Mary, Joseph, and baby Jesus
He'd pretend.

Lit the cherry bombs — Ka Boom!
Dressed the pumpkin.
"Merry Christmas!" Pookie hollered.
At least it was sumpthin'.

When suddenly to his surprise
Came a knock on the door.
Eight police cars,
Followed by more.

"We got a complaint about you,
You going to jail.
Ain't no use in resisting,
You po' and can't raise bail!"

Pookie started to cry.
Curled up like a mouse.
"Y'all having Christmas
Down at that jailhouse?"

"We've got turkey, pies,
taters, greens and cake.
Why you ask?
Did you light the bombs by mistake?"

"Oh no!" Pookie screamed,
Wiping the tears from his eyes.
"I think I should do time."
The police were surprised.

As they led Pookie away,
He turned around and smiled.
He winked at Mary, Joseph, and Jesus.
"Thank You. See y'all in a while."

On to the jailhouse, give me that turkey,
 pie, and cake.
Come on buttermilk biscuits, collards, and
 shakes.
Bring the lima beans, the ham, some
 stuffing, and more.
Pookie couldn't wait to get out the door.

Anyone else with good sense
Would have been annoyed.
But Pookie had been broke,
Hungry, busted, and unemployed.

Pookie finally had his Christmas,
Ate inside his jail cell.
He burped and belched a carol
It sounded like Noel.

They came the day after
To set Pookie free.
He punched out one cop,
kicked another in his knee.

"Oh no! He did not hit me!"
The poor cop whined.

"Oh yes, I did.
I guess I'll have to do more time."

"Lock that cell door!"
The cop started to bleed.
Pookie hollered real loud,
"What y'all serving New Year's Eve?"

Merry Christmas and a Happy New Year.
Remember, Jesus is the reason for the
    season.

"Pookie's Big Christmas"
by Pat G'Orge-Walker © 2002

BEA'S CHRISTMASTIME KEEP A MAN FRIED CABBAGE

First, it's Christmas, so wash ya dirty hands and go get ya some of this:

4 bacon slices
1 large head fresh cabbage, coarsely chopped (coarsely chopped means: of course it's chopped but not with an axe)
1 tsp. salt or a pinch
1 tsp. pepper or a pinch.

Now do this: Cook that bacon in a large skillet for about 10 minutes or until crispy or until ya get finish running yo mouth on the phone, getting all the dirt about Sasha Pray Onn's personal business from Alice "Grandma Puddin'." Take that bacon out (please use a fork instead of yo' hands. If ya don't know why, then ya ain't got no business cooking). Now put some salve on yo' burnt up fingers (if necessary) and drain the bacon on pieces of clean paper towels.

Keep 1 tablespoon of drippings (that's a fancy word for grease) in the skillet. Think about the one that done ya wrong and crumble up that bacon like that person's face is on it. Add the cabbage that ya stole (I'm sorry. That ya borrowed) from yo' neighbor's garden. Make sure you washed that cabbage first just in case yo' neighbor is trying to set ya up. Add to hot drippings (that's the grease I told ya about) in a skillet; sprinkle some salt and pepper. (If ya were feelin' a little lightheaded from that high blood pressure, then don't be so heavy-handed with that salt.)

Sauté cabbage (that means just cook it a little without burning it up) over a medium-high heat 10 to 12 minutes or until tender. (If ya like me, then y'all probably cook it in a little less time, 'cause the smell done made ya hungry.) Sprinkle on some of that crushed bacon.

Ya can only feed about 4 to 6 folks, so don't be running yo' mouth to folks about what ya cooking or ya ain't gonna have enough.

This dish takes about as long to put together as one of them television commercials: 10 min.

By the time ya get finished, ya done been in that kitchen cooking for about 20 minutes or so. It may be longer if ya waited till ya was ready to cook before ya stole that head of cabbage.

Hint: Use paper plates, so ya don't miss yo' soap opera, washing dishes.

DISCUSSION QUESTIONS

1. Has religion or necessity formed your opinion or practices regarding gambling?

2. Do you believe that anything regarding betting or gambling is sinful?

3. Do you believe the riches of the unrighteous are often stored for the righteous? If so, who or what is the basis?

4. We often believe that money is the root of all evil as quoted by many. Is that Biblical? If not, what does the Bible actually say that is misinterpreted?

5. Do you believe that riches (Biblically) refer only to money and precious metals or can it be something as basic as a borrowed tomb from a rich man? (Matt. 27:57–61)

6. Would you consider wealth a spiritual liability? (1 Tim.6:9)

7. Whose side do you take when it comes to the way Reverend Tom handled Trustee Noel? Has God ever dealt with you with a Peter revelation? (Acts 10:11)

8. Would you second-guess a leader who refused to accept help, whether financial or otherwise, if it were your church in need?

9. Sister Betty was a woman of wealth, albeit not a multimillionaire. She never seemed to forget there were others in need. Are you, or do you know of, someone with a similar regard?

10. Do you agree with Cheyenne's observation that Mothers Bea and Sasha were more alike than different? Do you know of any church members who fight and argue as much as these women? Are there any redeeming values or even hope for them?

11. Trustee Freddie Noel went through a subtle transformation. Did it make you think more or less of him? Do you believe

wealth brings about confidence, brings *out* confidence, or was the man delusional?

12. Did you think the seniors threw back too much at the Throwback Seniors Prom? What, when, how and why?

13. How do you feel about Sister Betty's impending nuptials? Do you believe it will happen or fall apart such as Bea and Elder Batty Brick's engagement?

14. Are there any character(s) you would like to have the author bring back? Who?